A Very Merry Christmas

Hawaiian Holiday Series

Denise Devine

USA Today Bestselling Author

Wild Prairie Rose Books

A Very Merry Christmas

Print Edition

Copyright 2018 by Denise Devine

www.deniseannettedevine.com

ISBN: 978-1-943124-15-2

Published in the United States of America

Wild Prairie Rose Books

Cover Design by Raine English

Sign up for ***Denise's Diary,*** my monthly newsletter at:

You'll be the first to know about new releases, sales and special events.

Special bonus story at the end of this book!

Passionate about sweet romance?

Want to be part of a fun group?

Visit us on Facebook at:

https://www.facebook.com/groups/HEAstories/

Introduction

Spend the holidays in Hawaii! Get ready for six weeks of romance with a new Christmas series brought to you by *USA Today* bestselling authors…

Hawaiian Holiday!

Six exciting, sweet novellas linked by a unifying theme. You'll want to read each one!

HAWAIIAN HOLIDAY SERIES

Six women set out on a twelve-day holiday getaway cruise to the Hawaiian Islands. Each woman decides to enjoy a beautiful, much-deserved holiday in an exotic locale and ends up unexpectedly finding love along the way.

This is A Very Merry Christmas…

Guess who's coming to dinner?

Sophie Lillie is looking forward to spending the holidays with her family on their annual Christmas cruise to Hawaii. It won't be the same this year, however, without her mother. Maggie's death has drawn the family closer together, but when Sophie's father shows up with his new fiancée at his side, their fragile reunion is torn apart. Sophie turns to an unlikely stranger for comfort, a man who is dealing with a betrayal of his own…

There's trouble brewing in paradise.

Sam Alexander's plan to turn a boring company cruise into a romantic getaway with a female coworker falls apart when she dumps him at the last minute for someone else. To make matters worse, his ex-girlfriend's new flame is Sam's workplace rival. He's stuck on a ship sailing to Hawaii with a bad attitude and nothing to do. That is until he meets Sophie, who melts his heart and gives him a reason to celebrate the season.

Find all the Hawaiian Holiday novellas at Amazon!

Christmas Charm by Raine English

Seashells & Mistletoe by Rachelle Ayala

Cruising into Christmas by Aileen Fish

Sunny Days Ahead by Julie Jarnagin

Aloha to Love by Josie Riviera

A Very Merry Christmas by Denise Devine

Chapter One

Day 1 – December 22nd

Sail Away

Sophie Lillie stared out the window of the limo, feeling like a kid again as she peered at the cruise ship docked at the Port of Los Angeles. She'd taken many cruises with her family and had sailed to exotic locations all over the world, but at twenty-nine, she still hadn't outgrown the rush of excitement that always filled her heart on the day of departure to a fun-filled destination.

"There's the *Bird of Paradise*," she said to her older sister, Dawn, as she gazed up at the imposing, fifteen-deck vessel with rows upon rows of rectangular windows gleaming in the December morning sun. Her father had booked their annual family Christmas cruise on this luxurious ship bound for the Hawaiian Islands. "Isn't it beautiful?"

Dawn paused, responding to Sophie's question with a cursory glance and a shrug, then went back to searching for something in her purse. "All cruise ships look the same to me—a huge, white box filled with too many people."

Sophie's older brother, Reid, snapped his laptop shut and grabbed his black, Under Armour backpack off the floor. "I'm looking forward to the food," he said as he shoved his computer into the large, square bag and zipped it shut. "Just thinking about it makes me hungry. As soon as we board, I'm heading for the buffet."

Dawn gave him an amused look. "You'll be standing in line with half of the people already on the ship. It'll be like feeding time at the zoo." Holding up her phone, she checked her appearance using her camera, tucking her straight, chin-length hair behind her ears. "I'm going to visit the spa and make appointments for a facial and a massage."

Sophie clutched her pink leather purse on her lap, thinking about what she wanted to explore on the ship. "The first thing I want to do after I drop my carry-on bag in my stateroom is check out the hot tubs." She looked at Dawn. "We'll need a nice place to relax after our morning workout."

"Workout?" Dawn countered with a droll grin as she slipped her phone back into her Louis Vuitton purse. "You're not getting me on a treadmill. The only heavy lifting I plan on doing for the next twelve days involves a wine glass."

The limo driver pulled open the passenger door and Sophie stepped out first, checking the time on her phone as she waited for Dawn and Reid. They were supposed to meet their father inside the terminal at one o'clock. She wondered if he'd already arrived or if he was still on his way from the airport.

She and her two siblings had flown in from Minneapolis a day early and stayed overnight in a hotel close to the terminal. Their father, Brad Lillie, had originally planned to join them there so they could all ride to the port together. Sophie didn't know why, but at the last minute, he'd suddenly changed his plans to arrive this morning instead.

They followed the driver to the back of the vehicle to retrieve their luggage, each suitcase equipped with a special tag provided by Aloha Cruise Line to ensure the baggage handlers loaded them onto the correct ship. The happy trio then handed their checked bags to a porter stationed curbside and proceeded into the terminal to meet their father.

Scores of people swarmed into the sprawling, noisy building. Cruise line staff stood at key points to direct passengers to their correct check-in locations. A large family pulling suitcases cut across Sophie's path and separated her from her siblings. She maneuvered around them as quickly as she could and glanced about, searching for her brother; a geeky-looking guy in his early thirties with thick, curly hair, a "Pink Floyd" t-shirt, sandals, and cargo shorts. Reid and Dawn both had the same tall, lean profiles as their father. Reid had sandy-colored hair like Brad, but Dawn's short locks were a tad lighter with a natural reddish tint.

They weren't easy to spot. By the time she'd located Reid, he and Dawn had blended into the maze-like check-in line for the *Bird of Paradise* and were slowly disappearing into the moving crowd. Obviously, they hadn't realized yet that she'd become separated from them.

"Reid!"

Reid and Dawn turned at the sound of her voice and vigorously waved at her to catch up to them. Sophie ducked under a black nylon rope and quickly joined them in line.

Dawn glanced at the time on her phone. "We should call Dad and coordinate where we're supposed to meet him." She scanned the organized chaos around them. "It's impossible to locate him in this place."

As if on cue, Reid's phone rang. "This is him now," Reid said as he lifted his iPhone to his ear. "Hey, Dad, what's up? Are you in the terminal or have you already boarded the ship?" After a brief conversation, he ended the call and shoved his phone back into the side pocket of his shorts. "Dad says he's running late. He'll meet us later at the *Sail Away* party."

A surge of apprehension filled Sophie's heart. She hadn't seen her father in months—six to be exact—and though she desperately wanted to make things right between them, the thought of facing him made her nervous. The last time they'd spoken was the day after her mother's funeral where their conversation had turned into a heated discussion over his disapproval of her boyfriend and her lifestyle. She'd refused to listen to his warning about Avery Newman and in defiance, walked out, stubbornly determined to do things her way.

It proved to be the biggest mistake of her life.

The *Bird of Paradise* would be at sea for three days before arriving at Hilo, Hawaii, on Christmas day. She planned to approach her dad tonight with a long-overdue father-daughter talk that she hoped would begin to repair their relationship. Christmas wouldn't be the same this year without her mother, Maggie, but Sophie still had her dad and she needed to make things right between them again by offering a sincere, heartfelt apology.

It took about fifteen minutes to reach the head of the line. A staff person quickly directed them to the next available representative to check them in. Sophie handed her boarding documents to the friendly dark-haired woman handling the process and received her "sea pass," a plastic card containing her picture and pertinent information. It served as her room key, her boarding pass, and a credit card aboard the ship.

Once they'd checked in, they headed across the terminal to enter the ship. A small crew of cruise line staff stood at the entrance to the covered gangway to take their "Welcome Aboard" picture. The female photographer stepped behind her tripod. "Smile!"

Sophie and her siblings stood together in front of a large poster of *The Bird of Paradise* with arms outstretched and wide, exaggerated grins.

The woman laughed as she pressed her finger on the shutter. "You guys have done this before, haven't you?"

"Every year since we were little," Reid said and grabbed his backpack off the floor. "Mom used the picture for her family Christmas card, but she's gone now, so…"

An awkward silence fell over the group.

Reid looked up. "I guess I'll give my copy to my girlfriend instead."

Dawn sniffled as she retrieved her carry-on bags off the floor. "Thank you."

"Check the photo kiosk on the ship tomorrow morning," the photographer said. "It will be ready for viewing by then."

Dawn signaled to Sophie and Reid to be on their way.

They walked across the gangway to the entrance of the ship. After they passed through the security line, they headed for the elevator bank and stood waiting for the next available car when Reid's phone rang again. This time the ringtone sounded different. His face lit up at the sound of Billy Joel singing "Uptown Girl."

"It's Ashley," Sophie whispered to Dawn, referring to the current love of Reid's life. "He told me this morning he changed her ringtone to that song because it reminds him of her."

Dawn rolled her eyes.

Sophie grinned.

Preoccupied with his call, Reid handed his backpack to Dawn and punched the elevator button to take him to the Hibiscus Star Buffet. Sophie and Dawn waved goodbye to him as they got off at Deck 8 to view their staterooms and drop off their small bags. All of their staterooms were next to one another on the "port" side of the ship, only a few doors away from the elevator bank and central stairwell.

Sophie entered her stateroom of taupe walls and matching carpeting. The long, spacious room had a large closet, a lighted vanity with a built-in desk, a cozy jade sofa, and a double bed. She set a small makeup bag on a corner shelf in the bathroom then walked through the room, dropping her purse and carry-on bag on the double bed on her way to the balcony. She pulled back the taupe and cream curtains in front of the sliding glass doors to let the golden December sun stream across the room. Opening the door, she stepped out onto the balcony and rested her elbows on the smooth, wooden rail, gazing at the deep blue waters of San Pedro Bay. A warm pacific breeze and the cawing of California gulls circling about the gentle waves created a mesmerizing backdrop that slowly began to relax her body and her mind.

"What's the matter?" From the balcony next door, Dawn's voice suddenly cut into her thoughts. "You look sad."

Sophie stared at the water and sighed.

Dawn leaned over the railing and tossed a cracker into the air. A white gull with gray wings and a black and white tail swooped down and caught it in midair. "Thinking about Mom?"

Sophie shook her head.

"Don't tell me you're obsessing about Avery Newman again."

Sophie shrugged.

"Look, Soph, you need to get over him. He used you, plain and simple. You're better off without that guy and you know it."

"I'm not obsessing over Avery." Sophie sighed again. Avery Newman had looks, talent, and an abundance of charm but no scruples. Leaning over the rail, she reached past the frosted glass partition that separated their balconies and held out her hand to take Dawn's box of snack crackers. "I'm thinking about the money and what I fool I was to trust him."

"Thanks to Dad, he didn't get a lot," Dawn said. Their mother had left each of her children a sizable trust fund, part of Maggie's inheritance from her parents. "Dad knew you'd be upset when you found out you were only receiving a small slice of your inheritance for now, but he believed he was doing the right thing. We all did."

Sophie blinked at this new revelation. "You mean you and Reid were in on it?"

Dawn gave her an incredulous look as she handed Sophie the cracker box. "Of course, we were. Dad wanted us unified on the matter before he talked to you. Reid and I agreed to receive the same amount that he gave you. Dad wanted to be fair."

Sophie laughed ruefully. "I accused him of being unfair anyway." She tossed a handful of crackers in the air to feed the growing number of gulls circling the area. "Why didn't you tell me this before?"

"Dad asked us to stay out of it." Dawn slipped on her sunglasses. "Besides, then you would have been mad at me, too."

Sophie tossed a couple more crackers to the gulls and handed the box back to her sister. She didn't want to talk about Avery anymore. Looking back, that portion of her life had played out like a bad reality show, one that she never wanted to take part in again. "Let's go and explore the ship," she said, turning her attention to their afternoon plans. "I'll go to the spa with you if you visit the fitness center with me. They're usually adjacent to one another."

"Okay, but the safety drill is at three-thirty and I want to come back here right after that so I have plenty of time to shower and change before the *Sail Away* party."

"Me, too," Sophie said, looking forward to twelve days of tropical fun. "I'm going to have a Mai Tai and enjoy the music. Let's get this party started!"

****

The *Sail Away* dance party started in the pool area on Deck 11 at 4:45 pm sharp. Sophie and Reid congregated in Dawn's room at 4:30 pm, looking over *The Coral Chronicle*, the ship's daily newsletter while waiting for Dawn to finish perfecting her makeup.

"Ah, c'mon, Dawn, it's a pool party, not the Academy Awards,"

13

Reid complained as he looked at his Apple watch. He still wore the same t-shirt and shorts he had on earlier. "We're going to be late and all the good appetizers will be gone."

"You just ate!" Sophie and Dawn exclaimed at the same time.

Reid adjusted his purple and gold Minnesota Vikings bill cap. "I heard there's going to be crab cakes and grilled shrimp on a skewer." He checked his watch again. "It starts in five minutes. Let's go!"

They arrived at the party just as a four-piece Hawaiian band with assorted drums, ukuleles, and steel guitars started to play. Sophie and Dawn parted company with Reid at the seafood appetizer buffet and made their way through the milling crowd to the poolside bar to get Mai Tais.

"This is just what I needed." Sophie sipped her fruity drink and tapped her foot to the ukulele. She wanted to dance but had no partner. Dawn wouldn't risk messing up her hair and Reid was too busy wolfing down his Hawaiian barbequed chicken to care about jumping around to the music.

Suddenly, someone grabbed her free hand and twirled her around.

"Ryan Scott!" Sophie burst into laughter as she whirled to the music. "What are you doing here?"

Ryan let go of her hand. "Getting away from the rat race, like you. Didn't you know we were here? I was looking for something different for our annual company bonus trip and Brad talked me into taking everyone on this cruise."

Brad Lillie leased all of his company cars from Ryan Scott's Mercedes dealership and had been a customer for years, long before Ryan had taken over the business from his father. Ryan and his father were clients of Brad's brokerage firm as well.

Sophie smiled. "Have you ever been on a cruise before?"

Ryan's brows deepened with apprehension. "Ah…no."

"Hey, there's nothing to worry about. The ship isn't going to sink." She patted him on the arm. "Believe me, you'll enjoy it so much you'll want to go again."

During her teenage years, Sophie had harbored a mighty crush on the tall, dark, and ruggedly handsome guy, but Ryan, who was five years older, had always been more interested in his snowmobile and talking football with Reid than flirting with her. However, they were both adults now, and perhaps…

Ryan grinned broadly. "Have you met my wife?"

My…*what*?

Sophie's smile froze as a petite blonde with long, layered hair walked toward them carrying a small plate of fresh veggies and fruit.

"Hi," the woman said warmly. "I'm Katie."

"H-hi." Sophie extended her free hand. "I'm pleased to meet you. How long have you been married?" *To the guy I used to dream about in high school…*

"Not long," Katie replied. "We tied the knot last summer on Enchanted Island."

"Oh, really? How was it? Enchanted Island, I mean." Sophie had only seen pictures of it online but knew that Enchanted Island was a beautiful, heart-shaped isle off the coast of Florida. "I've heard it's the newest, hottest thing for destination weddings."

Katie stared at Ryan with an adoring smile. "It was absolutely wonderful. I would recommend it to anyone in a heartbeat."

I don't have a future wedding to plan. I don't have a steady boyfriend or even know anyone I'd want to have coffee with, much less a date, Sophie thought glumly. Nowadays, her life consisted of her business and her cat. Since she'd broken up with Avery, she'd watched

15

more television than she had in her entire life. At least, it seemed like that, anyway.

The ship had begun slowly gliding out of the harbor. Sophie and Katie moved to the railing to watch the buildings along the oceanfront methodically slide by as the vessel began sailing across the vast waters of the Pacific Ocean to Hilo, Hawaii.

The band started to play on old Elvis hit, "Blue Hawaii." Sophie turned around and leaned against the railing, watching them play when something caught her eye or rather *someone.* A tall man with unruly blond hair approached Ryan wearing khaki shorts and a sky-blue polo shirt that emphasized his broad, muscular shoulders and arms.

Who is that?

Golden brows furrowed over deep blue eyes as the man spoke to Ryan. Sophie couldn't hear the conversation, but when Ryan shook his head in a manner that conveyed uncertainty, she wondered what they were discussing.

The breeze blew the man's thick, wavy hair across his forehead. He lifted his hand to brush it away and when he looked up, their gazes collided. For a moment, she couldn't look away, mesmerized by the intensity of his bold, confident stare.

Ryan spoke again, pulling the man's attention away, but that brief encounter sparked her curiosity. She had never seen the man before and wondered if he worked at Ryan's dealership. If so, the grim line of his mouth suggested something wasn't going right.

"Who is that guy talking to Ryan," she said to Katie.

"Oh, that's Sam," Katie replied matter-of-factly as she watched their conversation with interest. "Sam Alexander. He's one of our top sales consultants."

Katie joined Ryan to hear the conversation, leaving Sophie to sip her drink and wonder what was going on.

"Hello, Sophie."

She spun around the moment she recognized the deep timbre of her father's voice. Tall and slim with silver streaks in his sandy hair, he looked the same, yet something about him had unquestionably changed since the last time she had been with him. His eyes sparkled with purpose; his genuine smile widened effortlessly, creating a window into his frame of mind. She let out a sigh of relief, glad that he was happy to see her, but wondered what had happened to change his mind. Had Dawn given him a pep talk before the cruise and convinced him to let their disagreement go? If so, this was one occasion when Sophie didn't mind her big sister meddling in her affairs.

"Hi, Dad!" Ready to begin anew, she set her drink on a nearby table and fell into his outstretched arms, giving him a long-overdue hug as she sunk her cheek into his shoulder.

"I've missed you so much, honey," he murmured and wrapped his long arms around her, holding her tight. "I'm glad you're here."

In the corner of her eye, Sophie saw a female in her mid-forties, with shoulder-length blonde hair standing close behind him. Too close for a total stranger. The friendly, but tentative expression on the beautiful woman's face puzzled her. Sophie pulled back in surprise.

He turned his head and smiled at the woman then reached out and took her hand, urging her to come closer.

"Sophie," he said with a gentle note in his voice, "I'd like you to meet my fiancée, Carolyn Roberts."

His fiancée?

Sophie stared at the couple as her father's words sunk in. Mom had only been gone for six months. How could he forget his wife of nearly forty years so easily? And so quickly?

Carolyn made the first move, stretching out her hand. The huge diamond on her manicured finger sparkled in the light. "Hello, Sophie.

Brad has told me so much about you. I'm glad to finally meet you in person."

Stunned, Sophie mechanically held out her hand in response. "H-hello."

Carolyn's fingers clasped tightly around hers. "I realize this is quite a shock to you," she said kindly, "but I hope that we can become friends."

Sophie nodded, struggling for a reply. "How long have you been engaged?"

"Not long." Caroline marveled at her exquisite, marquis-shaped diamond engagement ring. "Brad proposed to me about a month ago. On my birthday." She looked up. "It was a delightful surprise."

"How long have you known him?"

"I had a couple of classes with him in college." Carolyn slipped her hand into Brad's. "We met up again a year ago at our college reunion party."

That was about the time Mom got sick...

Brad shifted nervously. "Would you ladies like a drink? Perhaps a glass of Cabernet?"

"I'll get it, Dad," Sophie said and backed away. The last thing she wanted was to be alone with Carolyn and struggle to make small talk. She needed time to process this new information. Did Dawn know about this? Why hadn't her sister warned her beforehand? Her heart ached with loneliness for her mom and she swallowed hard, missing Maggie more than ever as tears of frustration and profound disappointment rushed to her eyes.

Desperate to get away, she whirled around to head for the bar, but instead, she slammed into a man's chest. "I'm sorry," she said weakly as she wobbled backward and blinked furiously, attempting to clear the moisture blurring her vision. "I—I should have looked where I was going."

The man's strong hands gripped her to steady her. "It's my fault. I stepped in your way."

She looked up and found herself in the arms of Sam Alexander.

Chapter Two

Lost at Sea

Sam Alexander considered himself an expert on engaging with strangers, but he had absolutely no clue what to do with the weeping woman in his arms.

"Miss, are you okay?"

That's lame, Alexander. If she was okay she wouldn't be having a public meltdown...

Standing level with his chin, she gazed up at him through tearful brown eyes. "I'm fine. I just..."

"Would you like a glass of water or somewhere to sit down?"

She shook her head. "I'm okay. I'm going to the bar to get some wine."

He reluctantly let go of her. *Hmmm...maybe you've already had too much as it is.*

She must have read his thoughts for she sniffled and stepped back, putting a respectable distance between them. "I'm sorry. I don't usually wander around crying and crashing into people. I've just received some upsetting news."

Brad Lillie came up behind her and tapped her on the shoulder.

"I'll get the drinks, Sophie." Angling his head, he spoke close to her ear, but loud enough that Sam couldn't help but overhear. "While I'm gone, why don't you join your sister and visit with Carolyn? Make her feel welcome." He kissed her cheek and left for the bar.

Sophie wordlessly turned, her eyes filled with discomfort and uncertainty as she walked away.

"That's Brad Lillie's youngest daughter, Sophie," Ryan said after Sophie left. They watched her join the other women in their group. She stood silent, looking uncomfortable, and out of place.

Sam wondered what news she'd received that made her so upset she'd started to cry. That was no way to start a cruise. "We haven't been formally introduced, but I gathered that."

Ryan took a swig of his beer. "She doesn't look too happy right now, but she's a sweetheart once you get to know her."

His statement caught Sam by surprise. "How well do you know her?"

"We've been friends since we were kids." Ryan laughed. "She had a crush on me when she was in junior high. Followed me around like a puppy."

"Are you saying you didn't find that flattering?"

"Not really," Ryan said and took another swallow. "It was kind of annoying, to tell you the truth. I always thought of her as more of a kid sister than a girl I'd want to date. I actually had the hots for her older sister, Dawn. She and I were in the same graduating class."

Sam chortled. "Obviously, that didn't work out. What happened?"

"We started dating in our senior year, but it didn't last long." Ryan drew the bottle to his lips and drank the last few drops. "Dawn is a pretty headstrong woman. We were always butting heads over something." He pointed the tip of his bottle toward Sophie. "Sophie is just as independent as her sister, maybe even more so, but she's laidback, like Brad. I'll introduce you if you'd care to meet her."

Sam glanced at the girl and found himself inexplicably drawn to Sophie's silky dark hair, long and flowing to her slim waist. She had the face of an angel—heart-shaped with those big brown eyes and long, thick lashes. Her soft, full lips were perfect for kissing...

Lindsay suddenly invaded his thoughts, reminding him that he shouldn't be gawking at other women. He looked away. "I already have a girlfriend."

Lindsay McAndrews and he were both top earners in the sales division and had been awarded this cruise as a bonus. They'd been casually dating off and on for a while, but Sam wanted to find out if spending twelve idyllic days together in paradise would deepen their relationship. He'd made reservations in the ship's specialty restaurants for quiet dinners for two, purchased tickets to a wine-tasting event, and booked several shore excursions. He'd even ordered a bouquet and had them placed in her room before she arrived. He truly wanted this trip to be special for her.

Ryan shot Sam a sideways glance, raising one brow. "Now that you mention her, where is Lindsay?"

"She should be here any minute." Anxious, Sam shoved his hand into his shorts pocket and pulled out his phone. He'd been texting Lindsay all afternoon but hadn't received a single reply. After they'd boarded the ship, she'd complained of jet lag and had gone to her stateroom to take a nap. He hadn't heard from her since. Her silence had him worried. It wasn't like her to be offline for so long.

He swiped his phone and checked the screen. No word from her yet.

"Maybe she's changed her mind about coming to the party," Ryan said.

Sam shook his head adamantly. "Lindsay wouldn't do that without telling me."

Ryan raised his brows. "Are you sure?" He sounded dubious.

Sam did a double-take. Why would he ask that? "*Yeah*, I'm sure."

Ryan went silent after that and made a point of concentrating on his next beer.

Sam hung around for the duration of the party, not wanting to leave in case Lindsay showed up, but when everyone returned to their staterooms to get ready for dinner, he took the elevator to her stateroom instead. She didn't answer the door so he decided to canvass the shops on the Royal Promenade Deck to see if she'd simply gone shopping and lost track of the time.

The Royal Promenade, a two-story shopping and entertainment complex, encompassed the entire center of Decks 4 and 5. Sam stepped out of the glass elevator, next to a huge, two-story Christmas tree flocked in white with royal blue ornaments, and walked from one end of the ship to the other, checking out the retail shops, the café, coffee and ice cream vendors and several lounges. He saw garland, lights, and red velvet bows everywhere, but he didn't see Lindsay.

Frustrated, he went back to his room and changed into evening attire for dinner then went to Lindsay's room again and knocked on the door. No one answered. He tried again. Still no answer. Where could she be?

Maybe she's already gone down to dinner.

By the time he entered the Plumeria Dining Room, most of his coworkers had arrived and had already been seated. They cheered as he approached the table and made a toast to herald his late entrance. Sam ignored the laughter and multiple conversations going on around him as he made a note of two vacant chairs. Lindsay's seat—next to his—sat empty. And one other across the table; the one belonging to Derrick

Rossi.

"Sam…"

He turned to Ryan and saw the concerned look on the man's face. "What's going on?"

"Derrick sent me a text. He and Lindsay are…together. They're not going to make it to dinner."

For a moment, Sam entertained disbelief. He and Lindsay had talked about taking this trip together for weeks. Until now, she'd never had any interest in Derrick.

But he knew Derrick… The guy had a new girlfriend every other week.

His chest began to constrict at the thought of Lindsay getting sweet-talked by Derrick. His hands doubled into fists as heat crawled up the back of his neck. Grabbing his phone, he lifted his other hand to signal goodbye. "See you later. I've got a score to settle."

Ryan stood up and halted him with a gentle, but firm grip on his shoulder. "I know what you're thinking. Sit down, Sam. Take a deep breath. I need you to cool off and get your head on straight so you don't do something you'll regret."

Sam glared straight ahead, upset with Ryan's unwelcome interference.

"Look, I know you and Derrick have your differences—"

Sam's glare shifted in Ryan's direction, stopping him mid-sentence. "That's putting it mildly. He's just declared war as far as I'm concerned." He and Derrick were the top two sales consultants in the dealership. They had been workplace rivals since the day they were hired, but Derrick possessed a narcissistic streak that had caused a lot of friction between them. Derrick wasn't merely content to beat Sam at their monthly sales goals, he always made a point to publicly rub it in whenever he did.

They were arch-enemies now.

Ryan pulled out Sam's chair and gestured for him to sit. Despite his hurt and anger, Sam respected Ryan as both his boss and his friend, and though he didn't want to comply, he sat down.

A male server appeared at the table and spread Sam's napkin across his lap. "Would you like something from the bar, sir?"

Sam started to order a double shot of whiskey, but Ryan beat him to it.

"He'll take a Coke," Ryan said, cutting him off. "A *plain* Coke."

Once the server left, Ryan leaned toward him. "Sam," he said gravely, "I'm telling you this as a friend because I can see how upset you are and I know you're not thinking clearly." He leaned closer, keeping his voice low. "Give me your word that you won't say or do anything about this until you've had some time to calm down. Okay?"

Realizing the ugly truth, Sam looked Ryan in the eye. "You knew, didn't you?"

"I suspected it at the party," Ryan said evenly, "but I didn't know for sure."

"Why didn't you tell me?"

"It was none of my business." Ryan turned his back toward the table, presumably to keep their conversation private. "I don't get involved in the personal lives of my employees."

"Then what are you doing right now?"

Ryan looked around, making sure no one was listening. "I'm trying to prevent you from making a serious mistake that could spoil the cruise for the entire company. Hey, I'm not saying Derrick doesn't deserve to be confronted for what he did," he stated honestly. "If it were my girlfriend, I'd be anxious to even the score, too, but there's a time

25

and a place for payback and this isn't it, my friend. If you violate the code of conduct on your cruise agreement, you could be apprehended by security and spend the next three days in the brig. When we dock at Hilo, you'd be turned over to local law enforcement. You don't want that and neither do I."

Another server approached the table, handing a menu to each person. Ryan accepted the leatherette folder containing the day's dinner selections and laid it next to his plate. He waited until the server left then turned back to Sam. "I know I can count on you to do the right thing."

Sam thought about that for a moment. He exhaled a long sigh and ran his hand through his hair, thankful that Ryan had talked some sense into him before he'd gotten carried away and allowed his emotions to rule his head. Lyndsay should have been honest with him about her change of heart and though her betrayal had wounded his pride, he wasn't about to let it mess up his life. "You're right. She's not worth getting myself arrested and ruining everyone's cruise."

Just the same, Lindsay's thoughtless actions had already spoiled the cruise for *him*. He'd planned his entire trip around her. The reservations he'd made and the excursions he'd paid for would have to be canceled. The thought of following through on any of those activities by himself left a bad taste in his mouth.

It was going to be a long twelve days…

Sam stayed for dinner and tried to put it out of his mind by ordering his favorite food, a shrimp cocktail, and a T-bone steak. He even ordered a piece of chocolate cake for dessert. He didn't feel like attending the show, however. The thought of sitting in a huge theater full of people and laughing at some nutty comedian didn't appeal to him. Not tonight, anyway.

Midway through the meal, his phone pinged. It was a text from Lindsay.

Sorry about tonight.

He texted back… *Why didn't you meet me like we'd planned? Where r u?*

With Derrick. Will explain later.

Angry, he fired back another one. *I want some answers NOW.*

She went silent.

After dinner, he went back to his room to watch TV and deal with his low mood. The stress, anger, and humiliation that Lindsay had put him through had destroyed his ambition for the rest of the evening. Stretching out across his bed in his favorite gray sweatpants and t-shirt, he lay back against a stack of pillows and surfed through the channels.

A faint knock on the door awoke him. Lifting his head off the pillows, he looked around, realizing he'd dozed off. The knocking sound came again.

Sam shut off his TV and combed his thick, unruly hair with his fingers as he walked to the door. He expected to find Raoul, his stateroom attendant, waiting to turn down his bed for the night. He swung it open and froze, speechless.

Lindsay stood in the hallway, holding a vase of fresh flowers.

****

Lindsay McAndrews wore a long yellow dress with a round neckline and cap sleeves. Her thick, red hair, wound into a knot at the top of her head, had a small rhinestone butterfly clipped to a heavy curl, holding it in place. Her large jade eyes met his gaze. "I'm returning your flowers."

The way she held out the vase indicated she simply wanted to give him back the bouquet and go, but he stood aside and folded his arms. "Why? I sent them to you as a gift."

"I don't think we should see each other anymore," she said as she entered his stateroom. Her cheeks flushed with annoyance at having to bring the flowers into his room herself. "So, it's not right to keep them."

"If that's the way you feel, it's fine with me," he said, keeping his voice even. "I don't have time for a woman who can't be trusted anyway."

She set the vase on the vanity and whirled around. "I didn't cheat on you, Sam. We've had good times together, but I've always thought of you as a close friend, nothing more."

Is that so? If that was the best excuse she could muster, so be it. "Are you close friends with Derrick now, too?"

Her eyes flashed with defiance. "It's different with him." The tight lines around her mouth transformed into a dreamy smile. "I've finally found my soulmate."

For a week, maybe. Sam laughed mirthlessly. "When? Just today? Or have you been planning your little Hawaiian tryst behind my back?"

"No, it just happened, that's all." Indignant, she marched to the door. "I ran into him this afternoon in the café on the Promenade—completely by chance. We had a cup of coffee together and pretty soon he asked me to have a drink with him at the Irish pub. We ended up in his stateroom. He told me he's lonely. He wants to find a nice girl like me and settle down."

Sam almost choked. *That's the oldest line in the book...*

"You're making a mistake, Lindsay. You don't know Derrick like I do."

"You don't know him like *I* do." She clutched the door handle and looked back. "I'm sorry, Sam. I've let you down, but I need to follow my heart. You're a great guy, just not the one for me. I wish you all the best."

She wrenched open the door and walked out.

Sam grabbed the flowers out of the vase and strode to the sliding glass doors. Pulling open one side, he stepped onto the balcony, breathing in the balmy night air. A myriad of stars twinkled across the vast ebony sky. In the distance, lights from another cruise ship glowed like a golden beacon in the night.

He leaned against the railing and gazed down at the ocean. The whooshing sound of the ship cutting a path through the obsidian water filled his head like a mesmerizing song.

He tossed the flowers into the wind. A dozen pink roses cascaded through the air and disappeared into the night. He turned and went back into his stateroom, determined to get on with his life.

Chapter Three

Day 2 – December 23rd

Swing Time

"Tell me again why we have to do this."

Sophie stood in the elevator with her arms folded, leaning against the wall as she stared at Dawn, feeling mutinous. She had planned to work out first thing after breakfast, followed by a long soak in the hot tub then spend a few hours relaxing by the pool with a good book, but that obviously wouldn't happen now. Her morning itinerary for her first full day at sea had been hijacked.

"Because Dad *asked* us to," Dawn stated tersely once the elevator doors silently closed. The car began gliding up to the "Coconuts" disco lounge and observation deck. "He wants us to get to know Carolyn better and make her feel welcome."

"Yeah, but swing dance lessons?" Sophie unfolded her arms and gripped the handrail, clutching it to steady her nerves. "Why couldn't she have picked something fun and exciting like shopping or going to one of those diamond seminars? Swing dancing is for *old* people, not us."

Dawn watched the floor indicator light up the number for each deck as they rose to Deck 14. "I don't know why she picked that particular activity, but I promised Dad we'd be there." She glanced at her

30

watch. "We're late. I hope they didn't start without us."

The elevator came to a gliding stop and the doors whisked open. Dawn bolted out into the lobby and charged toward Coconuts with Sophie reluctantly trailing behind. They hurried into the lounge and found a large group of people spread across the dance floor, organized by couples. Brad waved them over to where he and Carolyn stood at the edge of the crowd, listening to the two dance instructors, Sergei and Natasha, give a brief summary of all the dance classes they would be teaching on the cruise.

Ryan and Katie stood next to Reid. Katie smiled, her eyes twinkling at the prospect of learning a new dance with Ryan.

"Hi, Dad," Sophie silently mouthed as she approached her father and his fiancée. Carolyn reached out and took Sophie's hand, squeezing it. "I'm glad you came. It's just getting started."

"It's about time you got here," Reid whispered to Dawn. "I need a partner."

Sophie suddenly realized she needed one as well. She looked around for someone to dance with, but everyone had a partner. There were no other singles there besides her. At first, she panicked. She couldn't swing dance alone. Then she smiled to herself, recognizing it as a blessing in disguise.

Good. I can sit this one out and simply watch from the bar.

Sophie raised her palms and shrugged, letting everyone know she didn't have a partner and therefore, couldn't participate. Relieved, she turned away to take a seat at the bar and sip a Diet Coke while everyone did their thing, but Dawn grabbed her by the arm and pulled her back.

"Oh, no, you don't," Dawn whispered. "I'll find someone for you."

Sophie folded her arms again and tapped her foot, seething at her big sister's second intrusion of the day. Who would Dawn find around here? The bartender? The maintenance man? Or did she plan to walk next door to the Diamondhead Lounge, the private club for elite members, and drag someone out to be Sophie's partner?

Suddenly, a tall, blonde man walked into the lounge dressed in running clothes and tennis shoes, heading straight for the bar. Dawn saw him the same time Sophie did, and her sister made a beeline for the man she'd run into at the party last night.

What's he doing up here this time of day?

Dawn approached him as he reached the bar and spoke to him, earnestly pointing to Sophie.

Oh my gosh, how embarrassing.

Sophie turned her back to them and stared at the instructors, hoping Sam had an excuse to get out of it. She saw Ryan making hand signals to Sam to join them and she cringed. Why couldn't everyone just leave her alone? Why did everyone have to be such meddling busybodies?

Dawn tapped her on the shoulder. Sophie slowly turned around, her hopes dashing. Sam stood next to Dawn, holding a slender bottle of still water, extracted from a glacial spring in Canada. It was a favorite beverage of runners, but only available on the ship at this particular lounge. "Here's your partner," Dawn said crisply and gestured toward Sam. "This is Sam Alexander. Remember him from the party? He works for Ryan." Dawn turned to Sophie. "Sam, this is my sister, Sophie."

Sophie greeted Sam with a nod then turned to her sister and murmured, *"Thanks."*

Wearing a satisfied smug, Dawn left them to make small talk with each other as she took her place next to Reid. Sophie stared after her, fuming.

"I don't want to be here anymore than you do so let's just do this and get it over with," Sam said quietly in her ear. "I'm no Fred Astaire, but don't worry, I won't step on your feet."

She looked up. Even though he wasn't in the best of moods, she still couldn't help noticing he had the bluest eyes, deep and rich like the color of the Pacific Ocean on a sunny day. His thick, blond hair and well-toned body made him one attractive guy and his looks probably gave him an advantage with many of the women who came to his dealership to buy a car. But that didn't mean *she* was going to drool all over him. She came on this cruise to forget a man, not pick up one. "I had other plans for this morning."

He held up his bottle of expensive water. "Me, too. I've got laps to run, but we're stuck now, so we might as well make the best of it."

"Have you ever tried to swing dance?"

"No." He frowned. "Have you?"

She shook her head.

"All right everyone," Natasha announced in her crisp Russian accent. The petite, dark-haired woman had a forceful voice for someone so small. "Let's get started. Now, there are many types of swing dancing, such as the East Coast Swing, the West Coast Swing, and the Lindy Hop, to name a few. Today, we are going to learn the East Coast Swing. We're going to teach you the basic steps so you can start dancing right away."

Sam set his water on a nearby table and stood side by side with Sophie, practicing the basic rock step and triple steps, keeping their knees bent slightly to create more fluidity in their movements.

"Rock, step, side-close-side, side-close-side," Natasha chanted. "Now do it again."

They practiced the steps individually until Sergei told them to join together as a couple. "Men, put your right hand in back of the lady on her shoulder blade. Ladies, put your left hand on your man's shoulder. Join your other hands together at waist level."

Sophie placed her left hand on Sam's shoulder, drawing in a sharp breath as he placed his hand on her back.

He looked down, his golden brows furrowed. "Is something wrong?"

"No, no I'm fine," Sophie blurted out, taken aback by the shock that coursed through her the moment his broad palm spread across her upper body. They stood stiffly facing each other, an arm's length between them. With joined hands, they waited for the instructors to give them the cue to start dancing without the music.

Sam's large hand gently squeezed hers and they began to step slowly, methodically, gradually turning in a circle as they went through the sequence over and over.

When the music came on, it took them by surprise. They both froze as people began to dance around them. Sophie stared up at Sam and they both burst out laughing.

"Rock, step, triple step, triple step..." Sergei rattled off over and over.

They waited until the sequence started again and began to dance, methodically moving to the count, making sure not to step on each other's feet.

"This isn't so bad," Sam said as he steadily guided her in a gradual circle. "I actually like this dance."

Sophie laughed. "You say that now, but wait until you have to start turning me."

Without warning, he lifted his arm and spun her in an outside turn. The sudden change in procedure made her lose her concentration and she tripped on her feet, slamming against him.

That's two times in two days. He must think I have the grace of a cow.

34

"Whoa," Sam said and wrapped his arms around her. "I don't want you to fall."

She stared up at him, her hands splayed on his chest. As their gazes melded, her heart began to flutter. "That was fun. Let's do it again." The words came out of her mouth before her brain caught up with her thoughts.

The instructors stopped the music and began to teach the rest of the class how to perform the outside and inside turns. Sophie and Sam placed their arms in the correct position and began to dance once more. Sam turned her slowly, enabling her to keep up the correct count as they rock stepped, twirled in six steps and rock stepped again, their bodies flowing in perfect harmony. The way he turned her and guided her around the floor with his strong, but gentle touch made her think of Belle dancing with the Beast in his castle. She smiled and laughed as she pivoted under his arm. She kept laughing until Sam stopped and pulled back.

He frowned, giving her the impression that he thought she was laughing at him. "What's so funny?"

"Look at my brother, Reid. He's stumbling around like he has two left feet and both legs in a cast."

Sam looked back at Reid and Dawn attempting to keep their steps in sync. He grinned at Sophie and they both laughed so hard that people began to stare at them.

Sophie couldn't remember the last time she'd enjoyed herself this much and she didn't want to stop when the music quit.

"Now you know how to swing dance. Good job, everyone. Thank you all for coming," Natasha said, indicating they'd completed the lesson. "We'll see you on the dance floor tonight at the disco!"

Many couples began to leave.

"I didn't expect to get sidetracked by a dancing lesson this morning, but I must admit, I enjoyed that." Sam retrieved his water off the table and began to make his way to the door. "You were a great partner and I hope you have fun at the disco tonight."

His eagerness to leave disappointed her at first. Then she realized she'd reacted hastily. She'd only encountered him twice and both times she'd nearly flattened him. They barely knew each other. Besides, she wasn't looking for a romance on the high seas. A guy this good-looking probably had a girlfriend or a wife anyway...

"Yikes, we've been here for thirty minutes," Dawn said looking at her watch. "I've got to hurry to The Lotus spa or I'm going to be late for my teeth whitening appointment. See you in the dining room for lunch at noon sharp. Don't be late."

Dawn followed Ryan and Katie out of the disco. Reid had already left to go rock climbing somewhere on the ship. Only Brad and Carolyn were left.

Brad smiled and slid his arm around Sophie's shoulders. "Did you have a good time, sweetheart?"

"Yeah, I did," Sophie said honestly, "but it went too fast."

And Prince Charming didn't stick around to escort me to the ball...

Carolyn smiled. "Will we see you at dinner tonight or do you have other plans?"

Sophie returned her smile, making an effort to warm up to the woman. "Yes, I'll be there. What time shall I meet up with you?"

"We're meeting in the lobby of the dining room at six-fifty. We've got reservations for seven." Carolyn slipped her arm around Brad. "It's formal night, so wear something sparkly!"

Sophie waved goodbye and left the disco, wondering what Sam Alexander would look like in a tuxedo...

A Very Merry Christmas

****

Sam exited the elevator at Deck 12 and headed to the center of the ship to get on the jogging track. He had enough time for about a dozen laps before he had to go back to his stateroom, shower, and change clothes before meeting Ryan for lunch.

Sam performed a few stretches and hit the track at a leisurely pace. The elevated track circled the deck one level above the outdoor swimming pool. He gazed down at the open area of the deck below as he made his way along the port side of the ship, noting all of the people sunning themselves on the rows and rows of deck chairs lined up on each side of the pool. A petite brunette with long, straight hair walked between the rows toward the fitness center. As if sensing his gaze upon her, she looked his way.

Sophie Lillie...

She stopped and waved at him.

He waved back and continued jogging until she disappeared from his line of sight. Beautiful and vivacious, Sophie Lillie was no ordinary woman. He couldn't deny that he'd had fun learning a new dance with her this morning and couldn't forget how perfectly she fit in his arms. Every time she'd looked into his eyes, his pulse sped up a notch. In another place and time, he would have pursued her without reservation, but after the way things ended with Lindsay, he needed some space.

He drew in the fresh, Pacific air and increased his speed. He had the next eleven days completely to himself. To his surprise, he never felt so free.

Chapter Four

Trouble in Paradise

Sophie met her family in the lobby of the Plumeria Dining Room for dinner at six-fifty, sharp, wearing a black sequin-covered chemise. During lunch, Dawn had mentioned the possibility of stopping by the portrait studio after dinner for a family photo so she wanted to look her best. Sadly, this would be their first time without Mom...

Her mood struck a melancholy cord, filling her with emptiness as she realized how much she missed her mother. Her heart ached with loneliness at the thought of enduring this cruise without her. Though Maggie's funeral had taken place last June, the memory of that tragic day still hurt as though it had happened yesterday. Sophie pushed the thought out of her mind. She knew she had to let it go or the sadness welling up in her would cast a pall on her holiday. Dwelling on it tonight would only serve to ruin her evening.

She walked through the main floor of the three-story dining room, passing table after table covered with white linen and seated with people dressed in their finest garb, enjoying the festive occasion. On a cruise of this length, there were usually two formal nights, one at the beginning and one at the end. Sophie loved them both but favored the latter night because one of the main entree choices would be lobster.

The center area of the huge formal dining room was open, floor to ceiling, revealing all three levels, and a massive crystal chandelier, supported by four white columns. Sophie made her way toward the far end, close to the grand staircase that led up to the second level. Everyone had already arrived and was seated at a round table near the staircase, sipping on glasses of wine. Dawn wore a full-length ivory dress covered with crystals and seed pearls. Next to her, Reid wore a gold T-shirt under a navy sports jacket. Sophie couldn't see the rest of him but knew he wore his usual khaki pants and his "good" tennis shoes. At the head of the table, her father looked stately in his black tuxedo. To his right, Carolyn sat in Mom's place wearing a close-fitting silver dress covered in Swarovski-like jewels that sparkled like a thousand points of light. Her shoulder-length blonde hair had been styled in a mass of curls atop her head. Her natural beauty and regal sense of style made it plan to see why Brad had been attracted to her. Still, it made Sophie sad to think her father could put aside the memory of his beloved wife so quickly and move on…

Their waiter, a young man from Romania, seated her at the empty chair next to her father, placed her napkin across her lap, and poured her a glass of red wine. She sat down, glad to be seated where she could foster conversation with him and begin to make up for the time they'd lost.

Brad raised his glass in a toast and glanced around the table. "To family." He turned to Carolyn. "And to a new beginning."

The clink of glasses touching and murmurs of well-wishing from Dawn and Reid followed his heartfelt proclamation. Sophie sipped her wine but remained silent. A new beginning? Yes, their family needed that, but with this being their first holiday without Mom, it seemed to her they were turning a corner too quickly.

Sophie smiled at no one in particular and busied herself drinking her wine. When the menus were distributed, she kept her head down, trying to shift her focus to the selection of entrees. She decided on a classic Caesar salad for her first course, chicken marsala, mashed

Denise Devine

potatoes, and buttered vegetables for her entrée. She paid little attention to what the others were ordering, but she couldn't resist exchanging a smile with Dawn when Reid picked two separate entrees for his main course—beef medallions with mashed potatoes *and* shrimp ravioli.

They were enjoying their coffee and dessert when Brad signaled for everyone's attention. He'd been his usual self through the meal and talked about the dinner reservations at specific places he'd booked for him and Carolyn when they reached Hawaii. Now, however, he seemed somewhat nervous, as though he'd pre-planned this part of the evening, but was unsure of how well it would be received.

Sophie exchanged looks with Dawn. *What's going on?*

Dawn met her gaze with a baffled look and a shrug.

"Kids," Brad said finally, applying the term he'd always used when addressing them as a group. "Carolyn and I have had a lot of discussions about our future and I've made a decision." The finality in his voice brought everyone up short. Dawn's face went into emotional lockdown, Reid's fork halted mid-air as the three of them waited for him to finish...

"I'm going to put the house up for sale."

Reid choked on his bread pudding alamode. Dawn's face drained whiter than her dress. Clearly, Sophie's siblings never saw this coming any more than she did.

Sophie cleared her throat, the first one to find her voice. "But, Dad," she said, sounding as perplexed as his announcement had left her. "Why do you want to move? We grew up in that house. All of our memories are there."

Brad nodded, acknowledging her reply with a swiftness that suggested he'd rehearsed this argument in his head repeatedly and had all his answers down pat. "I'm sorry, honey, but a five-bedroom house is too big for Carolyn and me. The maintenance on that place is expensive and too time-consuming. Once I retire, we plan to travel extensively so we're buying a townhome. Besides, honey," he said gently, "it's time to make new memories."

Sophie looked askance at Dawn and read the reaction on her face…

Translation: Wife number two doesn't want to take over a house filled with wall-to-wall reminders of wife number one.

Reid's jaw dropped, his eyes widening in panic mode. "That means I'll have to move. What am I going to do?"

Dawn gave him a disgusted look. "You'll get an apartment and pay rent like everyone else does."

"We're not waiting for the house to sell before we buy the townhome," Brad said. "We're closing on our new property right after Christmas, so there is no hurry."

Dawn pushed her dessert away and clutched her coffee cup with both hands. "What about Mom's things? Practically everything in the house belongs to her."

Sophie and her siblings waited expectantly.

Carolyn sat rigid with her hands in her lap, staring at Brad. Her discomfort over the family's emotional reaction to this permanent and obvious unsettling change was clearly evident in her rose-colored cheeks.

Beads of sweat formed on Brad's upper lip at the mention of removing Maggie's personal property. He hastily loosened his bow tie, as though he thought the thing might choke him. "You kids inherit it all. Maggie would have wanted her children to have her possessions." His gaze circled the table, embracing each child individually. "Including the profits from the sale."

Neither Sophie nor her siblings spoke as they absorbed this new revelation. The house didn't have a mortgage so the three-way split, along with their trust funds, would result in a nice nest egg for each of them. Her father had used the monetary gift as a peace offering, but Sophie didn't want it as much as she wanted to keep the house—and the memories of her mother—intact.

"Dawn, you're in charge," Brad continued. "I'll leave it completely up to you to coordinate cleaning out the property and disbursement of the contents with Sophie and Reid. When you're finished, I'll call my realtor to do a walk-through and make a note of the things that will need to be fixed or updated before he can list it."

The prospect of emptying their childhood home of all they held dear left Sophie sad and hollow inside. She dropped her napkin on the table and pushed back her chair. "Excuse me. I need to get some fresh air."

She left the group and made her way through the dining room, holding back her fragile emotions until she was totally alone. Once she'd passed through the Plumeria's wide doorway, she headed for the closest exit. The glass doors opened and she stepped out onto the promenade in the presence of a cloudy, windy night. A few enthusiastic souls passed her by, some taking a leisurely walk, others traversing at a fast clip. Some people were simply standing at the guardrail, enjoying a beautiful night at sea.

She began to stroll along the lighted walkway, lost in thought as the warm Pacific wind blustered around her, whipping stray hairs about her face. Her family home had served as the anchor that kept everyone tethered together after her mother died. Once they sold it, what would happen to their traditional get-togethers on holidays? Once her dad retired and started traveling extensively with Carolyn, would their family vacations cease?

A sudden gale of wind surged from behind, catching her unaware as it pushed her across the walkway, slamming her against the guardrail.

A man stood leaning against it, staring out to sea. Sophie reached out, grabbing the railing to avoid crashing into him.

"Excuse me," she said, breathless, as she held on for dear life. "The wind pushed me—"

The man turned at the sound of her voice and Sophie, once again, found herself staring into the compelling eyes of Sam Alexander. At least this time, thankfully, he didn't catch her blubbering like an idiot.

****

Sam blinked in surprise, recognizing the dark-haired woman in the sparkling dress. "Sophie? Are you okay?"

Her brown eyes widened with embarrassment at her near-crash landing. Colliding with objects seemed to be a regular pattern with her, or did it only happen around him?

"Hi, Sam." She smiled, blushing. "Yes, I'm…doing the best I can under the circumstances." Though she'd woven her hair into a thick braid, the blustery air had loosened a few tendrils, swirling them around her face. She looked like a windswept angel.

"It amazes me how we're always running into each other." *Literally*… "What are you doing out here this time of night by yourself?"

She clutched the railing with both hands as another gust of wind whipped around them. "Taking a walk."

His gaze dropped to her three-inch heels. "In those shoes?"

"I didn't intend to stay out here very long." She looked away. "I just needed some time to clear my head."

The tense thread in her voice signaled to his trained ear that something else had prompted her to brave this weather in high heels and a sequin dress that must have cost a small fortune. "Is everything okay?" he asked again, this time with more concern.

She went silent for a moment then sighed. "No, but I guess it's not the end of the world. Just the world as I once knew it."

Oh-oh.

He leaned one arm on the railing and angled toward her. "I don't know what your situation is, but I do understand what it's like to have things happen in your life that you can't control."

Sophie leaned against the railing and stared unhappily at the roaring waves down below. "If I told you my problem, you'd probably think of me as just a spoiled kid who can't be happy for anyone else."

"What I see is a woman who's deeply loyal to those she loves."

She looked into his eyes. "How did you know that?"

"I don't have any proof." He shrugged. "There's just something about you that gives me the impression you care deeply about the people around you."

"The person I care about the most is gone forever." She turned back to the railing and stared upward at the thick dark clouds in the nighttime sky. "My mom died six months ago from pancreatic cancer. She'd been sick for an entire year. At the end, she was so exhausted and in so much pain she couldn't have endured much more." She cast him a sideways glance. "Neither could we."

Sam covered her hand with his. "I'm so sorry about your mother. It was a sad day for all of us at the dealership when she passed away."

"Thank you. So, you knew about it?"

Sam nodded. "Ryan told the salesforce about Maggie and kept us up to date about her condition. I remember when we sent flowers and he and Katie attended the funeral."

"It's been a rough six months so I really looked forward to this cruise," Sophie continued. "I planned to have a lot of fun and spend some quality time with my dad. I figured he would be lost without Mom since this was his first Christmas alone, but when we met up at the Sail Away party, he introduced me to his new fiancée." She laughed cheerlessly, her disappointment ringing loud and clear. "I didn't even know he had a girlfriend, much less a love interest. It shocked me so much that I started to cry."

"Maybe he's lonely."

"I guess so," Sophie said sadly, "and I can't blame him for that, but he's taking things in a direction that has even Dawn and Reid upset now. Tonight, at dinner, he announced he's selling the house, and Dawn, Reid, and I are supposed to divide up all of Mom's things among ourselves." She swallowed hard. "He doesn't want anything to do with it."

Sam understood her pain and tried to tread softly. "Maybe it's too difficult for him."

"*Him?*" Sophie's eyes blazed. "What about us? Sam, there's a door jam in the house that has a mark and a date for every year of my life. And Dawn's and Reid's, too. And that's just one indication of how much of our lives are invested in that place. Don't you see? If the house goes, all of our memories of Mom and our childhood will go with it. What's next? Is my dad going to retire and move to Florida with his new wife?"

He wanted to assure her that her family wouldn't break up and would most likely establish new traditions, but the distress in her eyes made him realize it wouldn't help her to go there, at least not tonight. She needed comforting, not a lecture. Unfortunately, his hesitation made her come to the wrong conclusion.

"I'm sorry, Sam," she said as she stared up at him. "I didn't mean to burden you with my troubles."

"Hey," he said gently and clasped her hands in his, "what are dance partners for, anyway? If you can't tell me, who can you tell?"

His teasing made her laugh and as he watched her face transform from a sad frown to a beautiful smile, he realized how much he enjoyed her company.

"You know, I really looked forward to this cruise," she said wistfully. "I envisioned having so much fun. Now, I just want to get it over with and go home."

Sam prefaced his reply with a wry chuckle. "Believe me, I know exactly how you feel."

Her phone suddenly rang. She pulled it out of her purse but had to speak loudly over the roar of the wind and breaking waves. "Hi, Dawn." She paused, listening. "Okay. See you then."

She hung up and slipped the phone back into her shiny black purse. "I have to go. Dawn says everyone is on their way to the photo studio for a family picture."

With the wife-to-be...

She said goodbye with a wave and a wistful smile. "It's been nice talking to you, Sam, even if I *did* do all the talking." She started to walk away, then spun around. "If you're going to make the late seating for dinner, you'd better get a move on. It's formal night, you know."

He'd hoped she wouldn't ask that question. "I'm skipping all the pomp and circumstance tonight. I went up to the buffet for pizza instead." Ryan had pressed him to meet the group for dinner, but he'd declined.

"Pizza? You could have had steak or shrimp in the dining room," she said, staring at him in bafflement. "Why did you pass up such a fantastic meal for something you could eat all day at the pool bar?"

Because I don't feel like spending two hours watching my ex-girlfriend hang all over my worst enemy...

"I didn't feel like dressing up tonight. I thought I'd hit the track for a few laps instead." *And work off some steam.*

She pressed her hand against a large pillar to steady herself. "In

46

this wind? You must be a real diehard. That sounds like a lot more fun than posing for pictures, though."

That got a grin out of him. "You should try it. The ship has a nice jogging tra—"

"How about tomorrow morning?" she said seriously. "I mean, it's more fun when you have a partner. Someone to challenge you."

Her invitation surprised him and threw him off guard. After his disastrous breakup with Lindsay, he'd pushed the idea of female company completely off his radar—at least until after he got back to the states. "So, you're a jogger, too?"

"Every day," she declared proudly.

The idea of a jogging partner to challenge him to work harder sounded intriguing. Too intriguing to pass up. Besides, this might be a way to cheer her up and help her keep her mind off her family issues. "How does seven work for you? Or is that too early?"

"It's perfect. I'll meet you in front of the Sky High Bar. See you then!" The automatic glass doors swept open. She hurried inside the ship and disappeared.

We're just friends, he thought determinedly as he leaned his back against the railing. *Jogging partners, nothing more.* The last thing he needed right now was to get involved with another woman, even if it was only temporary.

Sam pushed himself away from the railing and went back inside. He'd planned to meet Ryan and Katie at the live show later at the Anthurium Theater but quickly changed his mind. He needed to shower and take it easy for the rest of the night. Tomorrow, early, he had to meet Sophie at the jogging track and he intended to be fully rested.

Suddenly, the cruise didn't seem so boring after all...

Chapter Five

Day 3 – December 24th

A Merry Little Christmas

The next morning, Sophie arrived at the Sky High Bar next to the jogging track at five minutes to seven and found Sam perched on one of the stools, waiting for her. Light blue jogging shorts, a white t-shirt, and Adidas running shoes showcased his well-toned muscular body. Two bottles of his favorite Canadian water sat side by side on the countertop.

His hesitation last night to accept her invitation made her wonder if he really wanted to exercise with her, but the handsome grin on his face this morning supplied her with all the proof she needed.

"Hi, Sam," she said cheerfully. "What a gorgeous morning. Quite a change from last night."

The clouds had dissipated, giving way to a clear blue sky. In the distance, the misty horizon spanned across the water as far as the eye could see. Golden shafts of sunlight streaked through the thin clouds, dawning a new day.

"This is my favorite time of day." Sam slid off the stool and handed her a water bottle. "Ready to roll?"

Sophie thanked him for the water. She'd been so focused on

getting to the track on time, she'd forgotten to bring some. She slipped it into her waist pack then joined Sam in a few "dynamic" stretching exercises to warm up their muscles for the twenty-minute session. They started on the large, double-lane track at a fast walk for one lap, staying in the right lane so other joggers could pass them by, but gradually increased their speed until they were moving at a brisk pace.

"Do you work at your dad's investment firm with Dawn and Reid?" Sam asked as they approached a rounded corner. "I have funds invested with the firm and I've worked with Dawn, but I don't recall ever speaking with you or seeing you at any of their client social functions."

Both Dawn and Reid held key positions in their family business. Dawn worked side by side with her father as a financial consultant and Reid managed the IT department.

"No way." Sophie laughed. "I follow my own path."

"Somehow I knew you were going to say that." Sam kept his attention focused on the track, but the amusing tone of his voice left no doubt he'd suspected all along she had no desire to fall in line with the rest of the family. What he probably *didn't* know, however, was the extent to which she'd fallen out...

"I could never spend eight hours a day sitting at a desk like they do," she continued. "How boring is that? I'm a creative person. I need a more stimulating atmosphere."

"So, are you a poet? A sculptor or an artist?"

She gazed across the calm expanse of water, noting the infinite line where the sapphire ocean met the vibrant blue sky. "Oh, I've dabbled in all three, and I still do once in a while, but my main area of interest is working with other creative people. I own an art gallery in St. Paul near Victoria and Grand where I showcase local artwork and crafts, especially pottery." She shot him a pointed, no-nonsense look. "And no, my father did *not* finance it. He was initially against it, but I built my business all by myself, starting in college with a rented garage until I had enough money and clientele to move into a better space."

"You must have quite a knack for working with people to do so well."

"You, too," Sophie stated as they jogged along. "Have you always sold cars for a living?"

"For the most part, yeah." They rounded another corner and passed by an elderly couple taking an early morning stroll. "I've always loved anything with four wheels. I started out detailing used cars in high school for a neighborhood dealer and liked working with vehicles so much that I convinced my boss to let me try my hand at selling them. I've been selling cars ever since."

"You must be doing well to earn this cruise as a bonus. What a great life you must have."

He laughed. "I was thinking the same thing about you."

The conversation waned as they concentrated on their task and continued in silence until they started the cool-down phase of their run.

"I could use some coffee," Sam announced as they began doing static exercises. "How about we grab a cup at Starbucks?"

"You must have read my mind." Sophie had plenty of time to shower and get ready to meet Dawn for lunch, so why not? "You're on. I'm desperate for some caffeine."

They took the elevator to the shops on the Royal Promenade Deck and found the Starbucks, taking their place at the end of a very long line. A staff person wearing a Santa suit went down the line, taking everyone's order as they listened to lively Christmas music. Eventually, Sam and Sophie had their Venti-sized coffees in hand.

"I enjoyed our workout," Sophie said, making conversation as they waited for the glass elevator in front of the Plumeria Dining room to stop at their level. "Same time tomorrow?"

"Sure," Sam said and sipped his coffee. "The ship is docking at Hilo, but I think we'll have time to get in a quick run before they open the gangway to let everyone go ashore."

"Oh, that's right. It's Christmas Day tomorrow." Sophie nearly forgot what day it was. Being on the ship often caused her to lose all track of time. "Dad says we're having Christmas Eve dinner tonight with Ryan, Katie, and your entire group. So, I guess I'll see you then."

"I'm looking forward to it." Sam raised his cup to make a toast. "To Christmas Eve."

Sophie touched the rim of her cup against his, excited about dinner and the entire evening. After their family gift opening, they were going to the Anthurium theater to watch a live presentation of *A Christmas Carol*.

The doors to the glass elevator opened.

Sophie and Sam froze.

A single couple stood in the center of the car, embroiled in a passionate kiss. With emotions running high—and hands roaming everywhere—they didn't realize the elevator had stopped much less that they had a captive audience.

"Excuse me," Sophie announced in a loud voice and held the door back with her hand. "Are you exiting on this floor?"

The couple reluctantly pulled apart. The woman, a tall, thin redhead wearing a light green sundress, flushed as her gaze first met Sophie's, but the moment she made eye contact with Sam, her demeanor changed. She nervously looked away, as though his presence made her uncomfortable. Sophie's head swiveled in Sam's direction. He stood rigid, glaring at the woman's companion, his expression hardening into a stone mask.

What's going on here?

The woman's partner, a handsome man with thick auburn hair, a blue silk shirt, and dark slacks, seemed to enjoy the chance encounter. A subtle sneer laced the corners of his smile as he grabbed his girlfriend by the hand and walked out of the elevator with her in tow. "Have a nice day," he said to Sam in a voice that sounded cheerful, but distinctly mocking, too.

Sam's fist clenched.

Sophie watched the exchange, worried that Sam's temper could burst any second. One good punch and Handsome Guy would be down for the count. To her relief, Sam kept his free hand at his side, but she sensed it took great effort for him to hold his anger in check.

Sophie and Sam took their places in the elevator. When the door closed, Sophie turned to him. "Who was *that*?"

"Lindsay and Derrick." Sam's hard expression hadn't changed as he stared straight ahead. "They're coworkers."

"Really? For coworkers, they weren't very friendly, especially Lindsay. She looked embarrassed, almost ashamed, that we saw them...kissing..."

I mean, groping each other...

"She and I used to date. It didn't work out."

Sophie kept her expression neutral, but her mind began to spin, weaving facts and impressions together, concocting a theory of what had happened between Sam and the couple. In reality, though, Sam's reaction made it easy to guess. Derrick, the good-looking guy accompanying Lindsay must have come between them. Given the way he taunted Sam in front of her, this guy Derrick not only considered it some sort of personal triumph, but he enjoyed rubbing it in as an extra measure of self-gratification. Wow—what a jerk.

But, why?

Though Sophie wanted to hear the whole story, she didn't know how to broach a subject that was extremely personal and, frankly, none of her business. One thing she did know—Lindsay had been a first-class fool to turn her back on Sam—especially for that guy she'd apparently hooked up with. Sophie knew his type and had no time for a man like him. The moment he saw her, his gaze had zeroed in on her like a laser, covering every inch of her curves in one expert sweep. A faithful, trustworthy man didn't look at other women *that* way.

The elevator doors whisked open on Deck 8. "Goodbye, Sam. See you at dinner."

He didn't reply, his stony expression indicating he was still upset.

She walked out, resolved to find out what happened—after he'd had time to cool down. In the meantime, she had some serious shopping to do for tonight. A new dress and a gift for Sam topped her list.

****

The grand staircase of the Plumeria Dining room had been decorated with pine boughs, gold ribbon, and large colorful ornaments. A tree flocked in white with multi-colored lights stood in the center of the room. The lights were low. Soft strains of Christmas music filled the air.

Sam arrived a few minutes early and took a seat, saving the chair next to him for Sophie.

A server appeared at his side. "Merry Christmas, sir. Would you like a glass of wine or a drink from the bar?"

Sam ordered a glass of wine for him and one for Sophie then set a small gift for her on the table above her napkin. He'd found the perfect item while browsing through the Promenade shops. After the way he'd acted in the elevator this afternoon, he needed to make amends. He hadn't meant to take out his anger at Derrick on anyone else and the way he'd shut Sophie out after that encounter had been unfortunate and unwarranted. He vowed to keep his feelings to himself from now on.

"Merry Christmas, Sam!"

He turned at the sound of her sweet voice. His jaw dropped.

Sophie came toward him wearing a full-length gown in burgundy velvet with long sleeves and a V-neck. The long skirt, slit on one side to the knee revealed a slender, curved leg. Her sleek, dark hair flowed to her waist.

Remembering his manners, he sprang from his seat and pulled out her chair. "*Hello*," he said, awestruck. "You look wonderful."

She gave him a beautiful smile. "Thank you." As she sat down, a server appeared at her side and spread her napkin across her lap. "What's this?" She placed her burgundy clutch purse on the table and picked up the small white box tied with a red satin bow. "Sam, did you—"

"Merry Christmas, Sophie." He placed his hand over her slender fingers. A surge of warmth spread across his chest. "It's a gift for my dance partner," he said with a wink.

"Shall I open it now or after dinner?"

Sam's fingers tugged on the bow. "I think you should open it now..."

Her eyes flashed with excitement as she pulled off the ribbon and removed the lid. Inside, she found a flip-flop sandal pendant in gold on an eighteen-inch chain. The straps on the tiny shoe were studded with diamonds. "Oh, my gosh, it's beautiful! Thank you!"

"It'll look even more beautiful on you." Sam took the necklace from her and fastened it around her neck. "It comes with a sincere apology," he murmured in her ear.

Her delicate brows puckered with confusion. "For what?"

The scent of Hawaiian White Ginger perfume surrounded her like an aura, distracting him, but he kept going. "For acting so ornery today.

I was angry with Derrick, not you."

"I knew it wasn't directed at me, so don't worry about it." She opened her purse and pulled out a small flat box, setting it in front of him. "I've got something for you, too."

He hadn't expected that. Curious, he opened the box and found a gold money clip with an uncirculated Kennedy half-dollar encased in it, exposing the reverse side with the presidential seal. The eagle on the seal had been layered in gold, making it stand out.

"Thank you, Sophie," he remarked with amazement. "How did you know I wanted this?"

"I had help." She laughed. "Ryan told me you guys were looking at them yesterday."

By this time, all of the places around the table were occupied and people were observing their tender moment with open curiosity, including Lindsay.

Sophie picked up her menu, holding the manila sheet in front of her face. "Don't look now, but someone is watching us."

"Everyone is curious about us," Sam said matter-of-factly. "They're used to seeing me with someone else."

Sophie lowered her menu and angled her head toward Lindsay. "Would it be rude of me to ask why you and she aren't together any longer?"

Sam shrugged. "She needed to follow her heart."

Lindsay leaned toward Derrick and kissed him as if to publicly flaunt their relationship.

"I can tell you exactly what she sees in a guy like that." Sophie set down her menu. "I know because I used to be like her." She let out a sigh of regret. "It took me a long time to realize life wasn't all about *me*, but when I got tangled up with a musician by the name of Avery

Newman, I received a sharp lesson in humility." She cleared her throat. "Betrayal sucks but it feels even worse when you realize your own stupidity allowed it to happen."

Sam pulled a wad of bills from his pocket and fastened his new money clip to them. "I can't imagine why you think that about yourself. You're anything but stupid."

She countered with a rueful laugh. "My friends told me to dump him. My dad hated him. I knew Avery wasn't good for me, but he flattered me by always telling me what I wanted to hear so I allowed his bad-boy looks and his never-ending supply of charm to dazzle me. We moved in together and he began to walk all over me even though I refused to see it. By the time I realized what a fool I'd been, Avery Newman had done more than just break my heart. He'd slept with my best friend. He'd cleaned out my bank account, too. Put the future of my gallery in jeopardy." She picked up her wine glass and absently twirled the stem between her fingers. "After that, I got my act together and steadily climbed out of my financial hole, but nothing could diminish my regret."

She shifted restlessly in her chair, looking anxious to put the past behind her.

"Hey, don't let it get you down," Sam murmured gently, resisting the urge to slide his arms around her and comfort her. "It's Christmas Eve. You're surrounded by friends and family."

"You're right." She held out her wine glass to touch rims with him. "To friends and family."

A little voice in his heart echoed what his head refused to acknowledge—he wanted to be more than friends with her. Then common sense prevailed, reminding him that because of his disappointing breakup with Lindsay, the last thing he needed right now was another relationship. The closest he'd ever get to Sophie Lillie was to be her dance partner.

A Very Merry Christmas

****

After dinner, Sophie said goodbye to the Scott party, including Sam, and gathered with her family in her father's executive loft suite. The fifteen-hundred square foot, dual-level living space had all the comforts of a luxurious home, including a private butler, a library, a baby grand piano, a wraparound balcony with a jacuzzi, and a patio bar for entertaining. The outside wall of the suite consisted of floor-to-ceiling windows to provide the occupants with a comprehensive, private view of the ocean.

The butler had decked the living room with a table centerpiece, garland, lights, and a decorated Christmas tree flocked in white. An assortment of gifts piled under the tree waited to be opened. Sophie and Dawn had gone shopping earlier that day and purchased the gifts they needed, including doing Reid's shopping for him. The friendly staff at the boutiques and jewelry stores had wrapped the gifts and delivered them to the suite later that afternoon.

They gathered around the tree with steaming mugs of spiced cider and opened their gifts.

At Dawn's urging, Sophie sat next to Carolyn on the sofa so they could open their gifts together. It was awkward at first because she didn't know what to say to her stepmom-to-be, but she was determined to get to know the woman better.

If Carolyn found the situation as uncomfortable as Sophie did, she didn't let on. She was gracious and warm, showing excitement at all the gifts she received. Sophie had no idea what to buy her father's fiancée, so she decided on jewelry—a common denominator with most women.

"I love jewelry," Carolyn said, fingering the aquamarine and sterling silver bangle bracelet she'd received from Sophie. "Thank you!" She put her arm around Sophie, giving her an affectionate squeeze. "I'll wear it to the theater tonight."

"Here, let me help you." Sophie slipped the bracelet around Carolyn's wrist and fastened the tongue clasp, happy that she'd made a little progress in making Carolyn feel like part of the family.

Sophie was enthralled with her gift from Carolyn and her father, even though it was obvious her dad had nothing to do with choosing it. He would never have given her a pink, silk nightie with satin ribbons woven along the V-neck and a matching robe. The soft, delicate garments were exquisitely beautiful and the French designer label indicated the outfit must have cost a bundle. Sophie made sure she let Carolyn and her father know how much she adored it.

At 9:30 pm the group went down to the Anthurium Theater to see the ship's live production of *A Christmas Carol*. Brad Lillie had a private box on the balcony, one of the many complimentary amenities that came with his suite. The box held a dozen people, yielding more empty seats than filled ones. Sophie snagged a seat next to Carolyn in the front row and watched the crowd below file into the auditorium. She sat on the end where an extra chair could fit for Sam. She saw him enter with a couple of his coworkers and waved to him, furiously, but the commotion of hundreds of people trying to find seats was so noisy and distracting that he didn't see her.

"I'll be right back!" she yelled to Reid on her way out of the booth. "*Don't* take my seat!"

She charged down the spiral staircase to the main floor and elbowed her way along the aisle until she came to the row where Sam sat in the middle, waiting for the performance to begin.

"Sam!"

She made her way along the row, profusely apologizing repeatedly for causing people to stand up to let her pass. By the time she reached him, he looked surprised but pleased to see her. "Why don't you come up to the balcony and sit with me?" She pointed toward the area where her family sat. "We've got a private box."

Sam glanced upward. "It looks full. Are you sure there's room for one more?"

Sophie turned around to see what he meant and saw Reid sitting in her seat, eating the platter of cookies the butler had placed on a small table in the back of the box. Her eyes narrowed as she caught Reid's eye. He stuffed another sugar cookie in his mouth and looked away, unconcerned.

She turned back. "Yes, there are plenty of seats behind my dope of a brother!"

Sam laughed and followed her out of the row, apologizing right along with her to all the people they had to squeeze by to get back to the aisle. He grabbed her hand and followed her through the auditorium to the staircase leading to the balcony. By the time they reached the box, the Cruise Director, Gabriella De Luca, was on stage in a sparkly gold dress and shoes, welcoming everyone to the show. Sophie and Sam grabbed ice-cold glasses of filtered water with fresh lemon slices off the table in the back and settled into the last row, just the two of them.

"How was your gift opening," Sam whispered.

"I had a great time. Carolyn loved the bracelet I gave her." She craned her neck to look back at the table housing the water pitcher and announced in a loud voice, "You know it would have been nice to have a cookie with my water, but *somebody* had to pig out and eat them *all*."

Dawn made a loud "Sh-h-h-h-!"

Reid turned his head, giving Sophie a sly grin.

Sophie retaliated, aiming a lemon slice at the back of Reid's head. "I couldn't help that. He's starting to get on my nerves," she whispered in Sam's ear. "What did you get for Christmas?"

He couldn't answer at first, beset with silent laughter. "Since we're all getting presents from our families when we get home," he whispered at last, "we decided to exchange gag gifts instead. It was hilarious. The best company get-together we've ever had."

Sophie leaned on the armrest, placing her chin on the heel of her hand. "And what did you get?" she silently mouthed.

"A talking toilet paper spindle."

She blinked, trying to envision what it looked like and more importantly, what it sounded like.

The house lights suddenly went down.

"I'll tell you about it later," he murmured.

As a hush spread over the audience and the sweeping red velvet curtain whisked upward, Sophie thought about the day Dawn dragged her to a dance class because Carolyn had requested it. If she hadn't been in the disco at that very moment, she'd have never encountered Sam— or developed a friendship with him. Indirectly, Carolyn had been responsible for bringing them together. Who'd have thought something good could have come from a lousy last-minute invitation to a dance lesson?

She settled back in her seat next to Sam as Ebenezer Scrooge emerged from the shadows on stage. She couldn't remember ever having this much fun on a cruise in her entire life. And they hadn't even arrived in Hawaii yet...

Chapter Six

Day 4 - December 25th – Hilo, Hawaii

Mele Kalikimaka

Daybreak silently slipped over the horizon forming a layer of bright crimson as Sophie and Sam jogged along the running track. They were the only people getting exercise this morning and it proved a refreshing change to have the track all to themselves.

Last evening, by the time Sophie had returned to her room, brushed her teeth, and fallen into bed it was after one in the morning. She didn't operate well on five hours of sleep after a busy day and her body struggled to keep up with Sam.

He, on the other hand, couldn't have been more chipper this fine morning. If he felt any fatigue at all, he didn't show it.

They rounded the corner and Sophie almost bumped into him.

He slowed down. "Let's take a breather."

They reduced their speed to a brisk walk.

"What's on the family agenda today?" Sam asked.

You mean, if I survive this wretched workout? A long, leisurely nap…

Sophie slowed and tried to catch her breath. "We're going to dinner at a seafood restaurant in Hilo. After that, I think we're coming back to the ship. It's Christmas Day. What else is there to do on a major holiday?"

Sam put his hands on his hips as he walked along. "Lots of things."

She copied his "hands-on-hips" thing and did her best to keep up with him. "Like what?"

"Oh, like the Waimea Christmas parade, the Nani Mau Gardens, and a helicopter ride around the Kilauea Volcano."

"Really? Two out of three sound pretty good."

He perused her with an amused twinkle in his eye. "I bet I can guess which one you tossed out. It's not as bad as it sounds. Do you want to go with me anyway?"

Of course, she wanted to go with him. His agenda sounded like a whole lot more fun than what her family had planned. The only problem was breaking the news to her dad. Would he be upset if she took off with Sam instead of going to Christmas dinner with him and Carolyn? She already knew the answer to that…

Early this morning, the ship had docked at the Hilo cruise port on the big island of Hawaii. Sophie couldn't see much of the city from the ship except for the long pier, metal buildings, a water tower, and rows upon rows of shipping containers. Off in the distance, however, she saw thick, verdant forests and tall, majestic mountains. She wanted to see more of Hilo than the view from the window of a fancy restaurant. "Yes, I'm in. Where do I meet you and when?"

He stopped walking and pulled out his water bottle. "The ship opens the gangway at ten." He checked his watch. "That leaves us approximately two and a half hours to finish up here, shower, change, and have breakfast before we leave."

"Great! How will we get to these places?"

Sam took a swig of water. "I've rented a car," he replied as he recapped the bottle. "I could have booked a tour from the ship, but driving myself will save a lot of time and we can set our own schedule. Sound good?"

"Sure does!"

****

An hour later, Sophie walked into her father's suite for a cup of strong morning coffee and a private chat. Carolyn met her at the door in white shorts and a peach blouse.

"Good morning!" Carolyn shut the door behind Sophie and followed her to the spacious living room. The vaulted ceiling and wall of windows rose to the top of the second level. Soft sunlight filled the entire suite, brightening the walnut-colored furniture and royal blue rugs. "You're up early, Sophie."

"I jog with a friend at sunrise." Sophie looked around. "Where's Dad?"

The butler, a short, dark-haired man in a black suit, offered her a cup of coffee and some breakfast. She turned down the meal but accepted the coffee.

"He's getting dressed," Carolyn said and glanced toward the open stairway to the second level. "He should be down in a couple of minutes—"

"Carolyn!" Brad's voice echoed from the master bedroom. "I can't find my new shirt..." He walked out of the bedroom and stood at the second-floor railing in his white bathrobe, gazing down at them. "Hi, Sophie." He smiled broadly. "What brings you here so early?"

Sophie accepted the coffee mug from the butler and gripped it with both hands. Might as well get it out there right away and face the music. "I'm not going to go with everyone to dinner today. I've accepted another invitation."

"What?" Brad thundered down the blue-carpeted stairs. "Another invitation? With *whom*? Why don't you want to have dinner with your family on Christmas?"

"It's not that I don't want to spend the holiday with you, Dad. I want to see the botanical gardens and watch the Christmas parade in downtown Hilo with Sam." She purposely left off the part about the helicopter ride. No need to get him upset any worse than he already was.

"Sam Alexander?" His forehead creased with concern. "Isn't he the one going out to the airport today for a helicopter ride around the *volcano*?"

How did he know that??

"No." Brad shook his head, his jaw taut. "No daughter of mine is going to get involved in a dangerous activity like flying over an active caldera!"

"*Dad*," Sophie shot back, raising her voice, "we're only going to skirt the rim, not fly over it. Look, I may be the baby of this family, but I'm not a baby anymore, okay? I'm twenty-nine years old and I can make my own decisions!"

"There's no need to fuss over this." Carolyn stepped between them. "Let it go, Brad. She's only young once, but she's certainly old enough to know what she's doing. She'll be all right."

"But, Carolyn," Brad replied, softening his voice considerably. "I wouldn't worry if she was going fishing or whale-watching. Flying around a volcano is a risky business."

"I've met Sam," Carolyn countered, "and I believe he's a responsible man." She placed her hand on the center of his chest. "Sophie will be all right, dear."

Brad exhaled a loud, troubled sigh.

Carolyn turned to Sophie. "Have a good time, honey. Let us know when you get back."

Sophie handed the cup back to the butler and kissed her dad on the cheek. "I'll text you some pictures!"

She practically skipped out of the suite, excited to meet Sam for breakfast.

****

Sam held Sophie's hand as they walked along the pier, making their way back to the ship. The setting sun had given way to a purple sky and the stars were beginning to twinkle in the heavens.

"I had a great time, but, boy, am I tired," Sophie murmured as they trudged along. "I don't think I'm even going to eat dinner."

Sam glanced at his watch. They'd been up now for twelve hours, going strong. After they met in the ship's buffet for a quick breakfast, they'd gone down to Deck 2 to disembark and pick up their rental car. From there, they drove to the Nani Mau Gardens and spent several hours wandering through the exhibits, gazing at a spectacular orchid garden, rare palms, and tropical fruit orchards. They had lunch at a small, family-owned seafood restaurant and afterward, drove to the Hilo airport to catch a helicopter ride to view the diverse array of volcanic formations throughout the area.

Sophie was nervous about riding in the noisy helicopter and had gripped his hand for dear life as it lifted off the ground, but once they reached the Kilauea Volcano, she forgot her fear and instead found herself riveted to the fascinating scene below; the ancient, steaming caldera and the "hot spot" lava plume.

The last stop on their itinerary was the Waimea Christmas Twilight Parade. They bought cups of hot chocolate and watched the procession of vehicles and floats, all decorated festively with colored lights. They'd dropped off the rental car and made it back to the ship before the 7 pm departure time.

"Hey, the night is young. Does this mean you don't want to go dancing tonight?" Sam teased.

"Oh, ha-ha," Sophie quipped. "My feet are sore and I feel like a zombie. I'll be lucky if I have enough energy to brush my teeth."

Sam chucked. "Yeah, me, too."

They reached the ship's gangway and walked under a canopy erected at the base where cruise line staff checked their Sea Passes and directed them to continue. At the top of the gangway, they entered the ship and were processed through the security checkpoint.

"What are you doing tomorrow?" Sam asked once they made it through security and stepped into the elevator.

"We're in Honolulu tomorrow, right?" At his nod, she continued, "I'm supposed to go with Dawn to Waikiki Beach. Then we're going to have lunch and do some shopping." She leaned back against the handrail and closed her eyes. "What are your plans?"

"I'm going to view the USS Arizona Memorial."

"Really?" Her eyes flew open. "Gosh, I'd rather do that than lay on the beach and get full of sand, but I'm already in the dog house for not showing up for dinner today."

"How about dinner tomorrow night?" He knew he shouldn't ask, but the words came out before the common-sense section of his brain caught up to his mouth. "I've got reservations at Santorini's Italian Bistro at seven." He'd initially made the reservation for him and Lindsay. Once his plans with her fell apart, he'd nearly forgotten about it. Asking Sophie to have dinner with him, however, was a bit more personal than jogging or watching an electric light parade.

"Okay." Her worn expression quickly brightened. "Dad and

Carolyn have been invited to dine with the ship's Captain so I'm on my own anyway. They're meeting with Captain Berg for a private cocktail reception and dinner at seven, too."

The elevator doors opened up on Deck 8 and they walked out. Sam's stateroom was on the starboard side of the ship. Sophie's stateroom was on the port side.

"See you at the track," they both said at the same time as they went their separate ways.

On the way to his stateroom, Sam passed by Lindsay and Derrick in the hallway. They'd clammed up as soon as they saw him, but he could tell by the stony looks on their faces they'd been arguing. He suddenly saw them for what they were; a couple of shallow, unhappy people.

He ignored them and kept going.

Chapter Seven

Day 5 – December 26th - Honolulu

Sun, Sand, and Santorino's

"Come on, Sophie!" Dawn stood in the clear, blue-green water at Waikiki Beach wearing a hot pink bikini, vigorously waving to get Sophie's attention. "Take my picture!"

Sophie groaned and rolled over on the blanket. She still hadn't fully recovered from her sightseeing trip yesterday and didn't feel like doing anything that involved using her brain, much less hand-and-eye coordination.

"Sophie!"

She slowly sat up and pulled her phone from her beach bag. Dawn ignored the kids splashing around her and smiled for the camera, striking a sexy pose. Sophie got a couple of quick shots and threw the phone back in her bag. Then, as an afterthought, she reached back inside and checked her text messages. No new messages—nothing from Sam.

With a disappointed sigh, she tossed the phone back into the bag again, slipped on her sunglasses, and stretched out on the blanket.

What's the big deal? You're going to see him tonight anyway.

He'd been on her mind all day. She'd gone to the beach with

Dawn like they'd planned, but her heart wasn't in it. The place she really wanted to be was touring the USS Arizona Memorial with Sam. She'd had so much fun yesterday and couldn't stop thinking about him.

After a few minutes, Dawn came out of the water. "I'll stay with the blanket so you can take a swim."

Sophie sighed and sat up. "It's too crowded out there. Besides, I hate getting splashed with saltwater."

"Got any more complaints?" Dawn grabbed a towel and wrapped it around her waist. "What's the matter with you, anyway? You act like you don't want to be here."

"Sam went to the USS Arizona Memorial. I really wanted to see it."

"I think it's time we had a talk about Sam," Dawn replied in a no-nonsense tone as she took her place next to Sophie. "Look, I know you're having some fun with him, but you need to realize it's not the same as dating a guy back home. A lot of people hook up on a cruise. It's often only temporary, you know?" She picked up her floppy-brimmed hat and positioned it on her head. "When the cruise ends, so does the relationship."

Sophie rolled her eyes. "We haven't *hooked up*. We're just friends."

"*So far…*" Dawn grabbed her bag and began to rummage through it. "Things could change." She stopped and looked up. "Listen, Soph, I just don't want you to make wrong assumptions about him and get hurt."

Sophie smacked her lips in a huff. "Quit with the know-it-all, big-sister advice, okay? I wasn't born yesterday. I'm not going to get hurt."

Dawn pinned her with a pointed stare. "That's exactly what you said about Avery."

****

At ten minutes to seven that evening, Sam stood outside Sophie's stateroom, ready to escort her to dinner. He'd barely rapped his knuckles on the door when it flew open and she stood before him, looking like a princess in a shimmering, sky-blue dress. The necklace he'd given her for Christmas adorned her long, slender neck. Her sleek, dark hair cascaded past her shoulders like a silk shawl.

It took a moment to find his voice. "Ready to go?"

"Yes," she said, her eyes sparkling with anticipation. She snatched her clutch purse and let the door shut behind her.

They arrived at Santorino's Italian Bistro on time and were seated at a table by the window. Sam selected a bottle of wine and waited silently as the server poured them each a glass.

"How was your day?" he asked once the server departed.

"Long and boring. Crowded with tourists." Soft lighting from the Tiffany-style lamp on their table reflected the healthy glow of her tanned face. "I love Waikiki Beach. It's a beautiful place to spend an afternoon. I'd have rather gone to the memorial with you, though. How was it?"

"Sobering," he replied honestly, "but it was worth the trip. I've wanted to visit it ever since I studied American history in high school."

After that, they spent a few minutes in companionable silence, studying their menus.

We've got the entire evening to ourselves, Sam thought as he scanned the day's featured items. *There's no hurry…*

"I missed you today," he said as they munched on their dinner salads. "I kept thinking about how much you would have enjoyed walking the grounds of the memorial with me. It's so refreshing to be with someone who shares so many of the same interests as I do."

Sophie set down her fork and placed her hand on the table. "I missed you, too."

As he gazed into her eyes, his hand slid across the linen-covered surface and touched hers. "We've got all day tomorrow," he said, twining their fingers together. "I have a special surprise planned. That is if you feel adventurous and want to do something different."

"Like what?" Her voice sounded eager, but the warmth of her hand and the knowing light in her eyes sent a silent message that her mind, like his, was distracted by the invisible sparks ricocheting between them.

"You and me," he said slowly. "We'll rent a Jeep and drive to Polihale State Park for the day." His hand closed over hers.

Her eyes widened. "I can't wait."

Suddenly, their server appeared at the table with their entrees on a huge tray.

"Excuse me," he said as he took away the salad plates and replaced them with steaming hot platters of lasagna. "Enjoy your meal."

The spell broken, they moved on to other topics as they ate their dinner. They were sipping decaf coffee and discussing possible choices on the dessert menu when Sophie's phone rang.

"That's odd," she said and flipped open her purse. "Why would someone be calling me this time of night? I hope nothing is wrong." She pulled out her phone and checked the screen. Her brows knitted together. "It's Reid." She slipped the phone to her ear. "Yeah, what's up?"

Her frown deepened. "Okay. I'll be right there." She disconnected the call and grabbed her purse. "I have to go. Dad's called a family meeting."

Sam found her abrupt departure disappointing. He'd planned to take a walk with her after dinner and talk about his plans for tomorrow. "Why? What's it about?"

She pushed back her chair and stood. "I don't know, but it sounds serious. I'll meet you at the track tomorrow. Same time?"

She waved and hurried out of the restaurant, not waiting for his reply.

****

The door to Brad's suite stood ajar, held open with one of Reid's size eleven tennis shoes. Sophie burst into the living room and stared at the members of her family, all sitting down, all waiting for her so they could begin the meeting.

Brad paced the room in his black tuxedo and stocking feet. His bowtie hung loosely from his neck, as though he'd hastily pulled it apart. He pointed to a leather sofa chair, motioning for Sophie to sit.

Sophie silently took her place, anxiously searching the faces of her siblings. Dawn's solemn countenance gave the impression she was at a funeral. Reid just looked confused. Carolyn sat quietly, her blank expression giving away nothing...

"Carolyn and I had dinner tonight with Captain Berg," Brad began as he walked toward the group.

Yeah, we already knew that. Get to the point, Dad.

"We had a very interesting conversation with him." Brad walked over to the sofa and stood behind it, placing his hands on Carolyn's shoulders. "To make a long story short, he's agreed to marry us." He drew in a tense breath and held up his hand to maintain silence, as though expecting instant opposition. "The wedding will be at two o'clock in the Starlight Chapel on December thirtieth."

For a moment, everyone sat in stunned silence.

Dawn's face went ghostly white. "Isn't this rushing things a bit? What about the business? What about us? You should have a signed prenup agreement in place first to protect our inheritance."

"Why?" Brad's face flushed, turning a dark shade of red. "Do

72

you think Carolyn's in a hurry to get her hands on my money? What if she has more money than I do? It just so happens her son is even more concerned about the situation than you are."

Carolyn slipped her hand over Brad's as she met his concerned look with her own. "My son is an attorney and his firm is composing certain agreements for us to sign when we return." She squeezed his fingers. "Matthew's not happy with me at the moment."

Dawn was the first sibling to remember her manners. She stood and took Carolyn's hand. "Congratulations, Carolyn, and to you, too, Dad. I wish you both all the happiness in the world."

Reid expressed an abbreviated version of what Dawn said and shook his father's hand.

Sophie sat in stunned silence. She wanted to be happy for her father and his fiancée, but at the same time, her heart was breaking. Everything was happening so fast—the fiancée, selling the house, the surprise wedding. Why was her dad in such a hurry to put Mom's memory behind him?

She didn't realize she was crying until her father stood over her, pulling her from the chair. He wrapped his arms around her and held her close. "I haven't forgotten Maggie," he whispered in her ear. "She'll always hold a special place in my heart. Just like you."

Chapter Eight

Day 6-7 – December 27-28 – Kauai & Maui

Left Behind

Early the next morning, the ship docked at the Port of Kauai and opened the gangway for passengers to disembark for the day.

Sophie and Sam picked up their Jeep at a local rental agency and jumped on Highway 50, winding through colorful towns and villages as they made their way to Polihale State Park. An hour later, the highway turned into a bumpy dirt road, the gateway to the park. They drove past old sugar cane fields until they came to a stunning, two-mile stretch of sandy beach.

The dry, sandy terrain provided little in the way of vegetation or shade, but the endless expanse of crystal blue water made up for what the area lacked in greenery.

They parked the Jeep and explored the area then spread a blanket for a picnic-style lunch at the southwestern edge of the beach. There, they found a lagoon that was sheltered from the waves and currents. According to the rental agency, this was the only safe place to swim.

Sophie wore a cream, one-piece swimsuit under a white lace "cover-up" sundress along with a floppy white hat to shield her from the sun. She pulled off her sundress and went into the water, being careful not to go out too deep. She simply wanted to take in the warm ocean water, as though she were soaking in a giant bathtub and didn't go deeper than her chest.

Sam followed her into the water and swam circles around her, splashing her occasionally.

After a while, he dove into the water and broke through the surface so close to her, they were but a breath apart. Circling his long arms around her waist, he pulled her close. "I've heard this is a favorite spot for the locals to camp out on the weekends."

The gentle pressure of his powerful arms pulling her against his muscular chest gave her heart a momentary flutter. She slid her arms around his neck. "A beach party with the locals sounds like fun, don't you think?"

"The sunsets here are stunning. When the sun starts to slip behind the horizon, the rays project against the rocks and light them up with color. Maybe we could come back here someday and see it for ourselves." He angled his head downward and brushed his lips against hers.

"I'd love that." She leaned into him and tightened her arms around his neck, allowing him to kiss her deeply. "Just the two of us."

Cupping her face with the palms of his hands, he lifted her chin upward, showing her more tenderness than she'd ever experienced before. "I'm glad we're the only ones here," he whispered in her ear. "It's so noisy and crowded on the ship. I love having you all to myself."

They stood in the water, kissing and holding each other close, shutting out the rest of the world until the sound of rain pulled them apart.

Sophie went still, listening to the steady plunking noise as large drops hit the water. She looked up and saw dark clouds moving across the sky. When they arrived at this beach, the sun was high above. Somewhere between having a picnic on the shore and getting into the water, the weather had begun to change, but she'd failed to notice it. Maybe because she'd been a little preoccupied...

Sam grabbed her by the hand and began to lead her out of the water. "We'd better get going before this storm breaks. I don't want to get caught on this dirt road when it starts pouring."

They made their way out of the water, gathered up their belongings, and scrambled into the vehicle. Sam turned the Jeep around and high-tailed it out of the park. They'd only driven a few miles down Highway 50 when something went wrong with the engine.

"What's happening?" Sophie cried as the vehicle began to sputter.

"I don't know," Sam said, as he drove the Jeep onto the side of the road. "It's been working fine until now." The engine light lit up on the dashboard. He tried to start it again, but it wouldn't turn over.

They sat in the vehicle, watching the rain cascade off the windshield, stunned at their misfortune.

Sam pulled out his phone and called the rental company. They agreed to send a tow truck right away. Since they were nearly an hour away, that meant Sam and Sophie had a bit of a wait.

An hour passed with no sign of the tow truck. Sam began to get restless. He called the rental company and they assured him it would be there soon. Another half-hour passed. "They'd better get here soon or we might not make it back to the ship on time."

The truth hit Sophie like a tsunami. "Oh my gosh. What will we do?"

Sam stared out the windshield. "Let's decide that if and when we have to."

Twenty minutes later, the red and blue lights of the tow truck came into view. Within fifteen minutes the Jeep had been hooked up and they were on their way.

But they didn't make it back to the pier on time.

They saw the ship gliding out of the harbor as the truck pulled up to the pier.

Sophie and Sam stood in the heavy mist, wondering what to do next.

****

"I'm sorry, Sophie," Sam said as he started up the substitute rental car the agency had provided them. "I should have paid more attention to the weather. If I had, we might have made it back before the ship sailed."

She looked up at him. "What do we do now?"

He pulled out onto the road and accelerated. "We're going to Lihue. Tomorrow we'll catch a hopper flight to Kona and meet the ship there. The rental company is paying for it and they'll foot the bill for a hotel, too—that is, if we can find one. This time of year, everything is booked solid."

They were on their way to Lihue when Sophie's phone rang. Sam winced, knowing her family was probably worried sick—or steaming mad.

She pulled out her phone and put it on speakerphone. "Hi, Reid."

"What do you think you're doing?" Reid sounded furious. "Dad's having a fit because you missed the ship. Or did you do it on purpose?"

"What?" Sophie shook her head in confusion. "No, I didn't do it on purpose! We had car trouble, Reid. Why would I do that?"

"So you two can get away...to be alone."

His insinuation was clearly understood. And it made Sam mad.

He grabbed the phone away from Sophie. "Hey, Reid. I heard

that and it's not cool, man. We had trouble with our Jeep on the way back from the park and because of the weather, it took the tow truck a long time to get to us. We're on our way to the airport now to book our flights and we'll catch up to the ship at the next port." He winked at Sophie. "In the meantime, don't worry. I'll take good care of your sister."

"You'd better, or you'll answer to me!"

Reid's protectiveness of Sophie made Sam smile. "I'll call Ryan and Brad after I talk to you and let them know what's happened."

"Don't worry about it," Reid said. "I'll talk to them. But if you don't show up—"

"Hey, we'll be there if I have to get a boat and row it myself."

Sam handed the phone back to Sophie after Reid hung up. "As soon as we get to Lihue, we'll start looking for a place to stay. I'll check on the airport hours so we can be the first in line tomorrow morning to get seats on the plane."

When they arrived in Lihue, they went from hotel to hotel, but couldn't find a vacancy anywhere. They ended up in an all-night coffee shop, sitting on a wicker loveseat by an electric fireplace, trying to stay awake. Sophie didn't last long. Once she fell asleep, Sam slipped his arm around her shoulders and held her close.

Throughout the night, he had a long time to think about the situation.

How did we get here? A couple of days ago, we were near-strangers stumbling all over each other on the dance floor. Now, I'm literally spending the night with her, holding her in my arms.

He was going to have fun explaining the situation to her father tomorrow morning. For now, he held her close, enjoying their time alone together. Someday they'd look back at this trip and laugh, but in the meantime, they needed to get back to the ship…

At four-thirty, Sam gently awoke Sophie and escorted her out to the car. They drove to the rental company's Lihue location, dropped off the car, and took the shuttle to the airport, arriving at five-thirty, just as the airport opened for the day. Then they had to wait until the ticket agents came on duty.

By the time they boarded the small plane bound for Kona, the ship had already docked in the harbor. Sam tried to sleep but he was too keyed up to relax. Thankfully, the flight was so short, it was over before he knew it.

Sophie called Reid from the cab on their way to the pier to let him know they'd arrived and what time they'd be back on the ship. They finally arrived and trudged up the gangway. Brad and Carolyn stood on the other side of the security checkpoint, waiting for them.

Sam went through the security line behind Sophie, rehearsing his apology.

Brad stood with his legs apart, arms folded across his chest. "What do you two have to say for yourselves?"

"I'm sorry," they said in unison.

"No, it was my fault," Sam said gravely. "I accept full responsibility for causing your daughter to miss the ship. I should have had better sense than to drive out to a wilderness park on the edge of nowhere without checking the weather first."

Brad opened his mouth to reply, but Carolyn waved her hands in the air and motioned for silence. "Look, there's no harm done, so why don't we just put this behind us?" Her gaze pivoted from Sophie to Sam. "You're both adults. It was an unfortunate situation, but you handled it just fine." She turned to Brad. "Now, let's all go have a drink and enjoy ourselves."

She's one cool lady, Sam thought to himself as they made their way to the elevator.

They had one drink before each couple went their separate ways. Sam and Sophie parted as they got off the elevator on Deck 8, but not before Sam pulled her into his arms and gave her a passionate kiss. "What are you doing later today?" he teased. "Want to go jogging?"

She answered him with a groan and tired eyes. "*Nothing.* I'm so tired I can barely see. I'd love to make plans with you, but I need to hibernate in my stateroom for the rest of the day. Call room service."

He placed his finger under her chin and kissed her goodbye. "Okay, sleepyhead. Go get some rest. I'll call you later about dinner."

Sam went to his room and took a shower to get rid of the salt from swimming in the ocean yesterday. Strangely, he didn't feel tired, but when he climbed under the covers and closed his eyes, everything began to fade out...

Chapter Nine

Day 8 – December 29th

Confessions

Sophie stood in the bathroom, putting the finishing touches on her makeup when she heard a knock on the door.

"I'm coming!"

Expecting it to be Sam, she added a couple of finishing swipes of mascara to her eyelashes before stepping out to answer the door. But when she swung it open, she didn't find him standing there.

It was Dawn.

"What are you doing here?"

Dawn brushed past her. "I'm happy to see you, too."

Sophie shut the door and followed her into the room. "I'm just surprised. I thought you'd be with Carolyn, picking out flowers or something."

"That's done." Dawn dropped her purse on the sofa and sat down, crossing her legs at the knee. "Carolyn took care of all the details back when you were gallivanting around Kauai with Sam and giving Dad another reason to stress over you." She picked a stray hair off the sofa and wrinkled her nose as she dropped it in the small trashcan under the glass and chrome coffee table.

"Me?" Sophie sat on the bed and folded her arms. "I don't know why you're trying to dump a guilt trip on me, Dawn, but I'm not buying it. Carolyn stuck up for me and what she told Dad is true. I'm an adult and I can handle my own life just fine."

"Carolyn is a good woman. She's the best thing that ever happened to Dad."

Sophie bristled. "I like Carolyn, too. I think she's a terrific person, but *Mom* was the best thing that ever happened to Dad."

Dawn gestured toward the patio door. "Can you open that thing and get some fresh air in here? This place smells like a cellar."

Losing patience, Sophie swung her legs over the bed and marched toward the sliding glass door. She pulled it open and immediately, the soft roar of the ocean invaded the room like a natural "white" sound.

"That's better."

Sophie climbed across the bed and rested her back against a row of fluffed bed pillows, hoping Dawn had finished nitpicking about the housekeeping of her room so they could get on to more pressing issues, such as the reason why she barged into Sophie's room in the first place.

"I think it's time we had a heart-to-heart talk," Dawn continued, "about a serious matter."

"You slept with Avery and you're here to get it off your chest."

Dawn's mouth gaped. "Oh, please. Don't make me gag."

Sophie laughed and threw a breath mint wrapped in cellophane at her sister.

Dawn started to talk again but hesitated, as though steeling herself for something unpleasant.

Sophie sat up straight. *What's going on? She never loses her nerve. Ever.*

"I don't know how to lessen the shock so I'll just tell it to you straight. Mom and Dad weren't the perfect couple that you've always believed them to be. At one point in their marriage, they had decided to get a divorce."

Sophie stared at Dawn, disbelieving her statement. "I never saw anything amiss between them."

"That's because they didn't *want* you to see it, Soph. You were Mom's last baby and she always tried to protect you…" Dawn shrugged her shoulders with resignation. "…from just about everything."

Sophie tried to recall any issues between her parents, even so much as a disagreement, but she couldn't pinpoint anything. "When did this happen?"

"Just before Mom got sick. The divorce was actually her idea."

"I don't believe that. She loved Dad!"

The leg crossed over Dawn's knee began to swing back and forth. "You can love someone but at the same time, lose your compatibility with them. Mom felt that she and Dad had grown apart. He had the business and she had a different life. She wanted to purchase an artist's loft and pursue her love of oil painting."

"If this is true, why didn't they tell me?"

Dawn's foot dance ceased. "They were going to, but then Mom found out she had terminal cancer, and Dad, being the gentleman that he is, refused to leave her. In view of the situation, they didn't think it necessary to upset you with the truth."

"So, why are you spilling your guts to me now? She's gone and it doesn't matter."

Dawn shifted on the cushions. "Because Dad has been seeing

Carolyn for over a year. He told me he met her at his last class reunion. When he found out she was a widow and she learned he was soon to be a widower, they started a relationship. It wasn't something he planned." She gestured with her hand. "It just happened."

A deep sadness grew in Sophie's heart, for her mom, her dad, and Carolyn, too. Why did life have to be so complicated? So cruel?

Dawn stood up. "Dad knows you're having a difficult time adjusting to Mom's passing and his engagement to Carolyn, but he doesn't know how to help you heal." Her green eyes reflected sadness. "It's distressing him at a time when he should be truly happy."

Sophie's eyes filled with tears. She'd never meant to hurt her dad over Avery, Mom, or Carolyn, but she had without knowing it. "What should I do?"

Dawn picked up her purse, looking truly uncomfortable with so much heart-rending emotion being bandied about. "Just be happy, that's all, for him and yourself."

Sophie wiped her tears, determined to put the past behind her and start anew with her father.

Dawn said goodbye and left, the door making a sharp click as it shut behind her.

Chapter Ten

Day 9 - December 30th

The Wedding

Sophie sat among a small group of people in the sunny chapel, whispering among themselves as they waited for the ceremony to begin. Dawn, Reid, and Sophie were seated in the first row. Behind them were Ryan, Katie, and Sam.

The cream furnishings were simple but elegant; a small platform for the bride and groom, twin column pedestals, one on each side with a blush floral arrangement of roses, lilies, and gardenias.

A collective hush swept the group as Captain Jorgen Berg entered the room. He stood at medium height, wearing a dark uniform, double-breasted with four gold stripes on the cuffs. His trim, white beard added to his distinguished look. He carried a leather-bound volume and solemnly stood on the platform, facing the guests.

Carolyn and Brad entered from the main door and walked toward the front, arm in arm. They quietly stood in front of Captain Berg. Carolyn wore a blush silk dress with a layered skirt. Her shoulder-length blonde hair had been swept back with tiny sprigs of baby's breath positioned behind her ears. She carried a nosegay of paperwhite narcissus. On her wrist hung the sterling silver aquamarine bracelet.

Sophie was perfectly fine until she saw the bracelet and knew that Carolyn had worn it expressly for her. Suddenly, all the emotions of grief and happiness she'd been holding back couldn't be contained any longer. She went very still, trying not to utter a sound as tears cascaded down her face. She missed her mother so much at that moment, longing to talk to Maggie and tell her that it was okay to go her own way. Her father looked so happy today and she was happy for him. She wanted him to live the rest of his life loving and being loved.

Through her tears, Sophie stole another look at the bracelet and knew Carolyn wanted to get close to her, not to take her mother's place but to be a friend.

A small sniffle escaped her nose. Dawn looked straight ahead but passed her a wad of tissues. Sophie took one and held it to her face, hoping no one else would notice. She didn't want to pull any attention from the ceremony to herself. Suddenly, a large, gentle hand slid over her shoulder. Long fingers gently squeezed her muscles.

Sam...

He'd been her rock ever since the second day on the ship, cheering her up, and treating her special. A small thought lingered in the back of her mind. Dawn's words...

When the cruise ends, so does the relationship.

"And now, by the power invested in me," Captain Berg said in a distinct Norwegian accent, "I pronounce you Mr. and Mrs. Bradford Lillie." The Captain smiled. "You may kiss the bride."

The group erupted in applause as Brad proudly but nervously kissed his new bride. They turned and faced the group, smiling.

Sophie burst into tears and flew into her father's arms, crushing his rose boutonniere. "Oh, Dad, I'm so happy for you!"

Carolyn slid her arm around Sophie and the trio hugged each other tightly.

Chapter Eleven

Day 10 – December 31st

Dance the Night Away

"How do I look?" Dawn twirled around in front of the mirror, wearing a rose-colored dress with a swirly skirt. Her tall, lithe figure looked absolutely stunning in the outfit, but Sophie saw no reason to gush over it and cause her sister's ego to swell any larger than it already was.

"I like it." Sophie studied Dawn in the mirror. "Are you getting dressed up for anyone in particular?"

Dawn's mouth curved in a tiny, secretive smile. "Possibly... I had a glass of wine last night with Christian Haugland, the Cruise Sales Manager and he said he'd meet me tonight in the disco."

"Ooooh," Sophie replied, getting dramatic. "Is this a budding romance?"

Dawn fussed with her blonde, chin-length hair. "No," she replied with a laugh, "just a prestigious date for New Year's Eve." She spun around again. "What do you have planned?"

"I have no idea." Sophie shrugged. "Sam said we'd talk about it over dinner. Multiple events are going on tonight and we haven't decided which one to attend."

Dawn grabbed her purse and headed for the door. "Well, if you come up to the disco, stop by my table."

I'm sure it will be crowded with a "who's who" group of people...

Sophie had on the same dress tonight that she wore on the first formal night, her black sequined chemise, only this time her necklace was a gold flip-flop sandal with diamond-studded straps.

Sam's usual knock rapped on her door.

She swung it open and twirled around for him like Dawn did, only this time she almost lost her balance in her high-heeled shoes and crashed into the bed. Sam caught her and bent her backward in a dramatic fashion. "How would you like to go dancing tonight?"

Sophie laughed. "Sure!"

He lifted her back to a standing position. "Okay, but I think you should wear some shorter heels. I wouldn't want you to spin out of control and end up wiping out a few people." He cleared his throat. "At least not in that dress."

Sophie found a lower pair of heels in her closet and exchanged them. She grabbed her black clutch and followed Sam out the door.

Dinner was a noisy affair. Everyone on the ship seemed to be in the dining room tonight, dressed to kill. Brad's group joined Ryan's group once more for a lively meal. After dinner, they all went up to the disco to join the party in progress.

The disc jockey played an oldie tune from the 70s and Sam pulled her out on the dance floor. Like they did in class, he put one arm on her shoulder and grabbed her fingers with his other hand. They went through the steps of the swing dance, a little rusty at first, but after a few sets of rock, step, triple step; triple step, they got the hang of it again and started moving fast, like Natasha and Sergei had shown them.

Throughout the evening, Sophie and Sam danced and laughed and danced some more. Sophie had the time of her life, but Dawn's warning kept replaying in the back of her head. Was this the real thing with Sam or was it just a convenient "cruise romance?"

At the end of the night, Sam walked her to her door but didn't ask to come in. He said he had an important meeting tomorrow afternoon and needed to get some sleep. He kissed her goodnight and announced he didn't want to jog in the morning, either. She pressed him to meet sometime after his meeting, but he merely waved goodbye.

"I'll call you," he said as he walked away.

Sophie watched him walk briskly down the hallway and disappear around the corner. The ship would be back in Los Angeles the day after tomorrow. Once it docked and the cruise was over, she wondered if she'd ever see him again.

Chapter Twelve

Day 11 – January 1st

A Day of Reckoning

Sam walked into the restaurant five minutes before noon and took his assigned seat at the table. A dozen people from the dealership were on the cruise and most of them had already arrived for the luncheon ceremony. All except Derrick and Lindsay.

Ryan had invited everyone to a special event in Pedro's Mexican Restaurant to give out the company's yearly awards, including the top sales consultant. He and Derrick were tied for first place, but only one person would get the award. Besides a wall plaque, the award included a cash bonus and a new Mercedes.

Ryan impatiently checked his watch. "I've given the staff orders to start serving lunch at noon sharp so we're not waiting for the latecomers."

"Sam," Ryan said in a business tone as he took his chair at the head of the table. "I'd like to move up the time of our meeting and sit down with you right after this is over. A one-on-one someplace private where we can talk freely. I have a proposal I'd like to discuss with you."

"Absolutely," Sam said, "name the place and I'll be there."

"Great. We'll talk again after lunch."

Sam was sipping a cold, refreshing margarita when the couple in question made their entrance five minutes past noon. They burst through the door laughing and holding hands, like a new bride and groom leaving the altar to start their new life together. Lindsay wore a flowing green sundress. Her shining, copper hair covered her arms in a thick cascade. Derrick wore a dark suit with a rose on the lapel. He'd combed his chestnut hair back, making him look more like The Godfather than a guy who sold cars for a living.

Sam glared at Derrick as he pulled out Lindsay's chair and then took his place at the table.

Only one of us is going to win this award and I'm betting on me.

Derrick ignored him and instead concentrated on ordering a drink, all the while still wearing that triumphant little smirk over luring Lindsay away from him. As if he cared…

When the server left, Derrick placed his arm across the back of Lindsay's chair. She stared dreamily into his dark eyes, prompting him to kiss her.

Way to go, guys. This isn't high school. You two deserve each other.

Ryan cleared his throat and shot the lovebirds a sideways glance; a subtle hint to knock off the PDA. He tapped his glass. "Attention everyone. I'd like to welcome you all to our annual awards luncheon. You've done an outstanding job this year and this cruise is a token of my and Katie's appreciation. I'll keep this short and sweet. We'll have lunch then I'll present the awards over dessert. Enjoy your meal."

Sam put all of his energy into eating his steak and shrimp fajitas, keeping to himself as the conversation buzzed around him. He was certain he'd earned the award for top sales consultant. Just the same, the suspense made his nerves jangle. Though he and Derrick were at a virtual dead heat, Sam had gone the extra mile this year, training new people and putting in many hours at the dealership's present favorite charity—Habitat for Humanity. Ryan took facts like that into account when making his decision and Sam knew he had a much better record than Derrick. Along with the award, he'd get a cash bonus and the keys to a new Mercedes. He had his eye on a bright red convertible.

The dishes had been cleared away, the staff had poured coffee, and were serving deep-fried ice cream for dessert when Ryan stood up and declared it was time to hand out awards. He had six in all, ranging from the mentor of the year to the top sales consultant. Everyone applauded as he handed out each one until he only had one left.

"This was a difficult decision," Ryan said gravely. "Both Sam and Derrick have had an excellent year." He glanced at each man. "I can only give it to one person, but I want you to know that I value each of you and your service equally. You are the backbone of our company. I applaud both of you and see great things for each of you in the coming year." He paused, as though it took great effort for him to continue. "The award goes to Derrick Rossi."

As the applause thundered around him, Sam sat like a statue, dumfounded. How…? Why…? He watched Ryan woodenly shake hands with Derrick, hand him the plaque, an envelope, and a set of blank keys, sensing something was amiss. Ryan didn't seem to have the enthusiasm he should have displayed as he patted Derrick on the shoulder and congratulated him. When he turned away, his practiced smile had the hardness of a stone, his shoulders were far too rigid.

Derrick tossed the keys in the air, caught them, and walked out with Lindsay on his arm. As they passed through the door, Derrick stopped and winked at Sam. "Tough luck, Sammy Boy. Maybe next year."

Sam's blood pressure hiked up more than a few notches. He stood, anxious to leave.

"I know you're disappointed, Sam." Ryan came toward him, his expression solemn. "But I have something else in mind for you. Why don't we take that table over in the corner?"

Sam picked his sunglasses off the table and slipped them into his shirt pocket. He had absolutely no desire to talk about work issues today, tomorrow, or any other day on the cruise. "Sure," he said with little interest. He'd listen to Ryan's proposal and excuse himself.

Right now, his attitude needed a drastic adjustment. After he and Ryan got through their meeting, he planned to find a quiet place to have a nice, stiff drink and think about a possible career change.

He followed Ryan to the table and sat down.

"So, here's the deal," Ryan said, getting right to the point. "I didn't give you the award because if I did and then offered you another position, it would look like favoritism and cause hard feelings among my staff, particularly Derrick."

Sam sat like a stone, letting the words bounce off him, waiting for Ryan to get his little spiel over with so he could leave.

"I'd like to offer you the position of General Manager." Ryan paused, waiting for his words to sink in.

Sam mentally shook the cobwebs out of his head. "You what?"

Ryan repeated the offer and wrote a figure on a cocktail napkin, sliding it across the table for Sam to see.

"But…General Manager is your job."

"I'm turning it over to you. Now that I own the business, I'm concentrating on other aspects of it and I don't have time to do both."

"Why me?" Sam asked, curious. "Why not Derrick?"

"Derrick is good at just what he does—selling cars, but he's not an organizer, like you, Sam, nor is he disciplined. He goes through his paycheck like water through a sieve; always looking for an advance before payday. His personal relationships are like a cheap soap opera." Ryan leaned forward. "I need someone trustworthy to take over for me. You've got a good rapport with the other employees. They respect you and like working with you."

Sam sat up straight and looked Ryan in the eye. "Eleven days ago, you had to talk me off the ledge when Derrick sweet-talked my girlfriend into telling me to take a hike. I almost made a serious mistake. Are you sure you trust me?"

"Hey," Ryan said, raising his palms. "You were upset, but you didn't act on those feelings. You used more restraint than I would have in the same situation. I specifically watched you to see what you'd do and I'm proud to say you passed with flying colors. Yes, I trust you."

Sam glanced down at the figure on the cocktail napkin and smiled. Instead of Derrick's workplace rival, he would be Derrick's boss. He'd have control over everything. Suddenly that award didn't look so important any longer because next year, he'd be the one giving it out.

He looked up and smiled. "It's a deal."

****

Sophie needed something to drink. She'd run out of water and decided to get a Coke. There was an Irish pub on the Promenade where she could get a nice cold glass with some ice.

The Promenade area was packed with sales tables, heaped high with scarves, hats, bags, purses, and t-shirts. Other tables were stocked with watches and costume jewelry. Sophie had to maneuver her way through hundreds of busy shoppers swarming the Promenade, looking for last-minute bargains to take home from the cruise.

She made her way into the Irish Pub and wove through a packed house to get to the bar. In one corner, a solo singer belted out Irish tunes. When she finally got up to the bar, she wished she'd gone up to the pool bar instead, but since she'd gotten this far, she might as well stay. She ordered her Coke and stood waiting for the bartender to pour it when suddenly she looked through the crowd and saw Sam with Lindsay sitting at a table in the opposite corner, huddled together. Lindsay had her head down, but Sophie couldn't see what she was doing because Sam had his arm around her in a protective way.

Something in the way he held her, shook Sophie to her core. There was a closeness and a level of affection between them that she'd never attained with him.

Then he kissed her.

He never really stopped caring about her. He just used me to pass the time until she got sick of Derrick and came back to him.

A wave of nausea settled in the pit of her stomach. She grabbed her Coke off the bar and headed out, hurrying as fast as she could go to make sure Sam didn't see her.

Wiping the moisture off her face with the back of her hand, Sophie worked her way through the crowd as she headed for the elevator. As luck would have it, she ran into Dawn at the elevator.

Dawn put her arm around Sophie. "What's wrong?"

"You were right. It was just a cruise romance. I saw Sam with his old girlfriend in the bar and they were closer than two peas in a pod."

"Come on," Dawn said, sounding like a protective big sister. "Let's go up to our rooms. After we set our bags out to be picked up, you can stay with me. We'll watch Hallmark movies and order room service."

"You know," Sophie said as she swallowed a lump in her throat. "I feel better already. I can go home now and not wonder if I'll never see him again. At least I won't be waiting for the call that will never come."

Sophie packed her bags, set them out in the hallway to be picked up by the cruise staff, and turned off her phone. She spent the rest of the night with Dawn and forced herself to put Sam permanently out of her mind.

The next morning, her family left the ship early and took a limo to the airport. They'd almost made it to their gate when Sophie heard a familiar voice calling her name, but she didn't turn around. She didn't want to be hurt all over again.

Not willing to give up, he followed her to the waiting area of their gate and walked up to her. "Sophie, why haven't you answered my calls or text messages? I stopped by your cabin on the ship several times and you wouldn't answer the door. What did I do wrong?"

"It was just a cruise romance, Sam. Why bother to say goodbye when it means nothing anyway?"

He blinked, looking totally baffled at her reply. "Is that all I was to you? A temporary distraction? What about the day we spent at Polihale Park? The night we spent huddled together in front of the fire in the coffee shop? Didn't that mean anything to you?"

She folded her arms and stood her ground. "It did until I saw you with Lindsay. Don't deny it, Sam. I saw you with her yesterday in the pub. You had your arms around her and *you kissed her.*"

"It's not what you think." He glanced around as if to make sure no one was listening—probably Lindsay. "I was consoling her, and for the record, I only kissed her forehead. Derrick dumped her on the last day of the cruise. He told her what you just told me, that it was only a temporary fling and now that the ship was docking in Los Angeles, it was over. She was devastated and I felt bad for her, but I had no intention of getting back with her. I told her at the beginning of the cruise that Derrick would use her and toss her away like yesterday's newspaper, but she didn't believe me. Now, she's nursing a broken heart. The worst part is that she's going to have to work with him every day." He shrugged. "I gave her a shoulder to cry on when she needed it, but she's on her own now and not my problem any longer. I'm only interested *in you*, Sophie.

You're all I've thought about since the day we met."

Sophie stared at him, wondering if all this was true. With Avery—no, but Sam was different. His distress seemed genuine.

"Sophie," he said and took her hands in his. "Think of all the fun we had—it wasn't just a fling for me. The moment you and I connected that day in the disco, I knew there was something special about you. When we started jogging, I told myself we were just friends, but it wasn't true. Deep down, I've always wanted it to be more." He pulled her close. "I don't want this to be the end of us. I don't want to lose you."

She bit her lip, mulling over his words. It felt so good to be close to him again. To hear his voice. She wanted to give him another chance to see where it led them. Deciding to go with her feelings, she responded with a timid smile. "I guess I *could* use a good dance partner."

Flashing a handsome grin, he pulled her close and kissed her deeply, letting her know that he'd happily accepted the offer.

The airline staff announced the last call for all zones.

"Sophie!"

Sophie pulled away. "Dawn's yelling at us. Come on, we'd better get going before they close the hatch and we miss our flight."

Sam picked up her carry-on bag and walked her to the jetway door to have their tickets scanned. "Hey, you'll never guess what happened to me yesterday. I got a promotion and a big raise. I think I'm going to buy a house. Do you want to help me shop for one?"

"Really?" Sophie laughed. "I know a fantastic place that's for sale..."

They walked down the jetway, talking about their future.

The End

Want more? Read the first chapter of my novels or get my complete book list at:

https://deniseannette.blogspot.com

~*~

Audiobooks Galore!

Romance, Suspense & Cozy Mystery

Check out this month's audiobooks on sale for $1.99

Do you like audiobooks? Many in the list above are available in audio!

Check out Denise's website for links to each audiobook.

https://www.deniseannettedevine.com

Narrated by Lorana L. Hoopes

Monthly sales!

So This is Christmas

Denise Devine

USA Today Bestselling Author

A Sweet Christmas Romance

Wild Prairie Rose Books

So This is Christmas

Print Edition

Copyright 2016 by Denise Devine

https://www.deniseannettedevine.com

Published in the United States of America

Wild Prairie Rose Books

Chapter One

Winter in Minnesota didn't rate high on my list of seasons, but I couldn't imagine spending Christmas anywhere else. The pristine landscape, the crisp, fresh air, and the rainbow-colored lights decorating snow-covered roofs reminded me of a Hallmark movie. I loved shopping at the Mall of America for gifts and watching the Holidazzle electric light parade in downtown Minneapolis, but my favorite event always happened on the second weekend in December. That's when I met up with my best friends for three days of good wine, more food than we could ever eat, and lots and lots of laughter. We'd grown up in the same northeast Minneapolis neighborhood—Ellie, Jeanette, Ginny, Sarah, and me—and through the years, were inseparable until our careers took us in different directions. Now that we'd hit our mid-thirties, it had become more difficult than ever to schedule a "girls only" weekend, but we'd made it a priority.

We always spent the weekend at Ellie Stone's family cabin in Breezy Point, Minnesota. Frankly, I didn't know why they called it a cabin. The multi-level monstrosity had six bedrooms, four baths, a den, two kitchens, and two living rooms. In the lower kitchen, the Stone family cooked all their meals. The upper kitchen, the one with the beautiful view of Pelican Lake, was called the "lounge" and they stocked it with plenty of booze.

I decided to drive up to Breezy Point a few days early this year. Ellie's family had always considered me "one of the bunch" and had no problem with my coming up ahead of time. I needed to take a break from my company, Annabelle Lee Photography, something I hadn't allowed myself to do for a long time. Lately, though, I'd begun to question the price of success. I had a thriving business, but the toll it placed on my life was slowly burning me out. The thought of spending four days alone in that big house with nothing to do but sip wine in front of a crackling fire would be good for me. It would also force me to give some serious thought to the dismal state of my love life.

I arrived at the house around noon on Monday. Driving up the snow-covered alley, I pulled into the back of the house and parked in the driveway in front of the tuck-under garage. Thankfully, Ellie had already arranged for someone to clear away the snow and shovel the sidewalks. I slid out of the car and drew in a deep breath of fresh county air, taking a much-needed stretch from the two-hour drive from Minneapolis. Even though the sun shone brightly in a clear blue sky, the temperature hovered around twenty degrees. Shivering, I grabbed my bag and the tote containing my four-week-old kitten and bounded up the cement stairway. The Stone family always hid a spare key under the planter next to the back door. I let myself in through the screen porch to the lower level kitchen and living room.

To my surprise, the room was toasty warm. Ellie must have remotely turned up the thermostat at the same time she turned off the alarm so I could enter the house without setting it off. The tote with my sleeping kitten fit on the seat of the rocking chair. The rest of my gear landed on the sofa across from the fireplace. I hung my coat in the closet then went straight to the bathroom to fill the tub and strip down to my undergarments. A nice soothing bath sounded like the perfect way to kick off my vacation.

Suddenly, a loud thumping noise echoed from inside one of the lower-level bedrooms. My heart slammed into overdrive as a frightening thought raced through my head.

Is there someone else in this house?

No time to get dressed—I grabbed the fuzzy yellow robe hanging on the back of the door and wrapped it around myself then peeked through a narrow crack in the opening. I didn't see anyone in the living room but finding the immediate area empty didn't bolster my courage. I needed to call 9-1-1 and my phone lay tucked in my purse across the room.

Now, what do I do? I can't lock myself in here and hope the intruder just goes away.

My brilliant, lightning-fast mind said, *"Get the phone. Run. Now."*

Slowly, I opened the door and crept out, hoping the rushing water from the bathtub faucet made enough noise to mask my footsteps. I scurried over to my purse and snatched the phone then made a beeline back to the bathroom. I swung the door open and almost made it inside when a large hand gripped my shoulder.

"A-h-h-h-h-h!" The shrill scream shot out of me so fast I hardly knew I'd opened my mouth. My body shuddered and the phone went flying as the strong hand pivoted me, bringing me face-to-face with my aggressor.

My breath caught in my throat as the fear gripping me transformed into jaw-clenching anger.

"*Christopher Stone!* You scared me half to death! What are you doing sneaking around the house?"

I hadn't spoken to Chris since twelfth grade, but the gap in time did nothing to cool my foaming-at-the-mouth resentment of the kid who'd spent the better part of his youth teasing me.

Ellie's twin brother stood before me wearing nothing but a pair of skin-tight jeans, barely zipped with the top snap gaping open. I'd seen him wearing less at the beach, but even his favorite chino shorts had never looked this good on him. Before I knew it, my gaze quickly traveled from his slim waist to the width of his broad shoulders and smooth, muscular chest. Embarrassed by my obvious curiosity, I looked away. This body did not match the scrawny kid I used to wrangle with growing up. When did all this happen? I mean, I knew most ballplayers worked out to gain strength and boost their power to hit a baseball. I'd watched Chris on television and the big screen at Target Field, the Minnesota Twins ballpark, but I never imagined him looking this good up close...

He didn't seem to care about his half-naked appearance as he yawned and ran a hand through his tousled dark hair. "I wasn't sneaking around," he said in a smooth, deep voice. "I was sleeping. You woke me up."

I glared at him to mask the sudden flutter in my stomach. "Are you—are you alone?"

"W-h-a-a-a... of course, I'm alone."

I stared boldly into his deep blue eyes. "What are you doing here?"

He shrugged. "What I always do when I need to get away from the crowds—I crash at the cabin. What are *you* doing here, Annabelle?"

"This weekend is our annual girls' Christmas get-together," I said matter-of-factly and raised one brow to let him know he'd better crash somewhere else.

He frowned. "Aren't you a little early? It's only Monday. Ellie said you girls wouldn't be here until the weekend."

"No, I'm not *early*. I volunteered to do the pre-party housecleaning and put up the decorations so the place would look festive when everyone arrives," I said lying through my teeth. He didn't need to know my *real* plans.

"Okay, great." He sounded amused as he leaned over and picked up my phone. "I thought for a minute there you were trying to get rid of me."

My patience wore thin. "Look, Chris, you're going to be in the way. Don't you have to get back to the twin cities to get ready for a hot date with your new girlfriend or something?" *Whoever she is this week...*

He didn't rise to the bait, but I noticed a muscle twitch in his cheek, as though the whole "date" situation didn't sit well with him. It didn't surprise me considering the high-profile women he chased— Hollywood starlets, models, and pop singers—Queen Bee Central. He changed girlfriends with the same frequency most men took their shirts to the laundry. Okay, that might be a slight exaggeration, but just the same...

"Tell you what, I'll stay in my room while you vacuum and do whatever it is you need to do." His eyes flashed when I adamantly shook my head. "What's your problem?"

"It's not what, it's who." I took my phone from his hand. "I'm not in the mood to spend the next four days dodging a guy who likes to play practical jokes on me. You know, like throwing water balloons at me, unscrewing the top off the salt and pepper shakers, flipping my glass of soda upside down on the table, hiding a whoopee cushion under a blanket on my chair," and his crowning achievement, "putting a *live snake* down my shirt?"

He burst out laughing. "Are you still mad about that? I did those things when we were kids."

The fact that he *still* thought them funny *still* made me mad and I didn't trust him one bit. "You bet I am," I said in my snippiest voice, "and I'm soooo not in the mood for any of your antics this week."

"I'll be good." He held up both hands. "I won't cause an ounce of trouble. I promise." His gaze suddenly dropped to the front of my body and his eyes widened. "Uh, but I can't say the same for you."

I looked down and found my robe gaping open, my pink with black polka dot Victoria's Secret undies in full view. "A-h-h-h-h-h!" My scream this time had more to do with frustration than fright. I jerked my robe shut and stormed into the bathroom, determined not to give my childhood nemesis the satisfaction of seeing my face turn crimson like he had done so often in the past.

His triumphant laughter propelled me all the way.

Chapter Two

I emerged from the bathroom wearing black sweatpants and an oversized T-shirt with *Grandma's Marathon* printed on the front. After that embarrassing disaster with Ellie's bathrobe, I decided to play it safe with something baggy and boring. Chris had probably already come up with a dozen ways he could use the incident to tease me. He didn't need any more fuel added to the fire of his aggravating sense of humor.

Speaking of fire, I found a robust blaze going in the fireplace when I walked into the living room. Chris stood at the stove in the kitchen dishing up spaghetti. He still had on the same jeans, but he'd covered his well-developed chest with a black "Grateful Dead World Tour" logo T-shirt. He didn't mention my wardrobe malfunction when our gazes met, but the twinkle in his eye told me he still found it amusing.

You'd better not say a word, mister. Not if you plan to stick around for a few days...

"Hey, there, sunshine," Chris said, holding out a plate of spaghetti and meatballs. He always called me "sunshine" because of my blonde hair. He also occasionally referred to me as the "Brown-Eyed Girl" because of my chocolate-colored eyes. "Are you hungry? I made lunch."

"It smells good. Thank you." The sight of food made my stomach growl. I accepted the plate and grabbed utensils from the silverware drawer. "You always were good in the kitchen, weren't you?" I bit my lip, realizing I'd unwittingly opened the door for him to twist my words and tell me what he was *really* good at in the kitchen. A guy like Chris always had a comeback, and always used every opportunity that came his way to get under my skin.

Instead, however, he surprised me with only a handsome smile, showing off the results of two years of braces in junior high. "I baked some garlic bread, too. Help yourself," he said and pulled a metal cookie pan from the oven filled with a half-dozen slices toasted to a golden brown.

A strange howling made us both pause. I turned and stared at the back door. "What was that? It sounds like it's coming from the screen porch."

"It's probably Rex. I'll be right back."

I stood, plate in hand, taking my time selecting a piece of garlic toast when something large and furry bounded into the kitchen. It leaped toward me, placing its huge paws on my chest. The impact knocked me backward against the center island. The plate flew from my hand and crashed to the floor. "Chris! Oh, my gosh! Chris!"

I tried to get away but lost my footing when I slipped on the spaghetti and landed on the hard linoleum. Lying on my back, I stared helplessly into the dark, almond eyes of an enormous German shepherd. I tried to catch my breath as the monster devoured my spaghetti. Then he had the audacity to lick my face with his long, sticky tongue as if to thank me!

Chris burst around the corner, his eyes widening at the sight of me flailing about, struggling to get the dog off my chest. "Rex! Come here!" He grabbed his four-legged monster by the collar and pulled him away. "Annabelle, are you all right?"

"I-I think so." My head spun as Chris knelt and helped me sit up. "It all happened so fast."

"I'm so sorry about this." He put his arm around me and pulled me to my feet. "I should have warned you about Rex. He's not mean, but he *is* strong. I've only had him for a month. Been meaning to get him set up with obedience classes, but I've been so busy, I haven't had time."

Something in the way his muscular arm rested on my waist triggered all of my senses to go on high alert. He pulled me close, tucking my right shoulder into the hollow spot under his arm, pressing me against the length of his body. Unable to form a coherent thought, I took a deep breath and found myself even more distracted by the sharp, spicy aroma of his cologne.

"Feeling better?" His deep, throaty voice purred in my ear.

He had no idea...

The thought threw me off guard, making me uneasy. He and I had never been friends, only contentious adversaries. I pulled away and reached for a paper towel. "I'd better get the floor cleaned."

"I'll take care of this. Maybe you should go and wash your face." He took the paper towel from my hands, pursing his lips to suppress a grin.

I left him to handle the messy floor and went into the bathroom. One look in the mirror told me what he meant. My ponytail sat askew on my head with hunks of blonde hair pulled loose. My bangs were sticking out as though a tornado had whipped them around my face. Scarlet blotches dotted my cheeks and the tip of my nose where Rex's tongue had swiped me. Yikes! If my mind hadn't been so off-kilter from my encounter with Chris, I would have laughed myself silly. Instead, I ran the water and washed my face.

The kitten's frightened cries made me quickly forget all about my disheveled looks. I ran into the living room and found Rex with his black muzzle shoved deep into the tote bag. I imagined those huge fangs in his mouth taking a bite out of my baby and instantly I became as protective as a mama bear. "Rex! Get away from there!"

I stomped over to the tote and pulled his head out. My kitten mewled as I snatched up the bag and headed for the kitchen. Rex followed me, emitting a high-pitched whine. He watched me place the bag on the counter and sat in front of it, staring with his ears perked, as though waiting for a favorite dog treat. I pulled out the black and gray tiger kitten and checked him over. He seemed unharmed. With a sigh of relief, I placed him back into the tote.

Chris threw my broken plate into the garbage and turned around, curiously peering into the bag. "I wondered what you had in there. It started making noise when you were taking a bath, but I didn't think you wanted me digging through your personal things so I left it alone."

"I didn't plan to have a cat," I said as I pulled open the refrigerator door and took out a plastic container of milk. "The other day I stopped at a convenience mart near my house to fill up my car and when I went into the store to get a bottle of Diet Pepsi, I saw a box on the counter with a 'Free Kittens' sign." I opened the overhead cabinet and selected a saucer. "I brought my bottle to the cashier and noticed this kitten curled up like a snail in the center of the box, all by himself. All of the others had been sold. He looked so cold and vulnerable that my heart melted. I couldn't leave him there."

"That's sweet of you, Annabelle," Chris said and took the milk from me. He twisted the cap off and poured a couple of drops into the saucer. "You've always been a kind-hearted person."

I blinked. Did my ears deceive me, or did Christopher Stone just compliment me?

He placed the saucer in the microwave and programmed it for ten seconds. The bell went off and he pulled it out. "Here you go, little guy." After testing the milk's temperature with his finger, he set the saucer inside the tote. "What is his name?"

"He doesn't have one, yet," I replied with a tinge of guilt. "I've been so busy getting things wrapped up at work before I drove up here, I didn't have time to think about it."

I pushed the tote under the cabinet to discourage Rex's inquiring mind and helped myself to another plate of pasta. Rex followed me to the table.

"I can't believe how long it's been since we've seen each other," Chris said as he pulled up a chair and sat down. He extracted his iPhone from his back pocket and laid it on the table. It immediately began to chirp. He glanced at the screen and then ignored it. "How have you been? Life must be treating you well. You look great."

Another compliment, I thought, *and an all-time record for civility with me*. I didn't know what to make of it, but I decided to play along and see how long it lasted.

"Thank you. I'm managing my own photography studio. I specialize in weddings. My calendar is crazy busy spring through fall, but during the winter when business is slow, I do family portraits and headshots."

And I drag my PR materials to one bridal fair after another, meeting with prospective clients to fill my calendar for the next season.

Trying to stay afloat financially during the winter months proved as stressful as the eight to fourteen-hour days during the wedding season, but he didn't need to know that. He also didn't need to know the difficulty I had wearing so many hats—bookkeeper, marketer, graphic designer, customer service, secretarial, and pretty much anything else that needed my attention. Just thinking about it made me exhausted. I hoped a couple of days of rest would restore my vitality before my friends showed up on Friday to party non-stop over the weekend.

Rex slipped his head under my elbow and tried to get his nose into my spaghetti again.

"Rex, go lay down!" Chris gave me an apologetic look. "Sorry about that. His former owners never taught him anything useful."

I watched as Rex slunk away and lay down next to the rocking chair, sulking. "You should call him T-Rex. He's big enough. Where did you get him?"

"I rescued him from a family who lives about a block from Mom and Dad's house," Chris said as his iPhone chirped again. "I'd go by there every day and see Rex chained to a doghouse. When the first snow fell, I knew I had to do something about it and I approached the people, offering to buy him. As it turned out, the woman who owned him didn't want him anyway. She gave him to me."

"That's sad," I said and looked at Rex with a new attitude. He lay with his head on his paws, staring at Chris with a wounded look in his eyes. "Without training, he's mentally still a puppy."

Chris nodded. "Pretty much." He glanced at his iPhone again then shoved it aside. "So, did you—by any chance—bring your camera?"

I paused, my fork mid-air. "I always bring my camera everywhere I go. I thought I'd get some shots of the sunrise and the sunset up here. Why, do you want me to take some professional shots of you?"

"No." He shrugged. "I just thought it would be nice to have a quality photo of Rex."

"Sure," I replied as I twirled my spaghetti on a spoon. "How about you and Rex together?"

He didn't object, so I made a mental note to check the house for a place with decent lighting to get a good shot.

"So, how about you?" I asked and took a small bite out of my garlic toast. "How are things going in your life? I try to get to a Twins game as often as I can, but baseball season pretty much mirrors the wedding season, so it's tough to get to Target Field." In truth, I hadn't been to a baseball game in years. I quickly added it to my mental list of things in my life that needed to change.

"I always take a couple of weeks at the start of the off-season to hang out with Mom and Dad," Chris said and speared a meatball with his fork. "Right now, I'm involved in several non-profit events. Most of them are to raise money for youth sports programs. I like working with kids."

"What's your favorite event," I said, genuinely interested. I knew local sports figures participated in a lot of fundraising, but I had no idea what he did in that arena.

"Actually, it's this Friday." He grabbed a jar of grated cheese and shook it on his spaghetti. "I'm making the rounds at Children's Hospital with a couple of teammates. We're giving gifts to all the kids—a stuffed bear wearing a Twins shirt, some candy, and signed baseball cards." He looked up. "For me, it's the best day of the entire year."

"That sounds very rewarding," I said and wondered what it would be like to attend an event like that with him. "The kids must love it, too."

He sighed. "It's tough to see so many sick children, especially the ones in the cancer ward, but if I can brighten their day even a little, it's worth it. I'd like to have a couple of my own someday and I'd be grateful if someone did that for mine. Do you have kids?"

I don't know why, but the question made me uncomfortable. I shifted in my chair. "No, I'm not married."

"Wow. That surprises the heck out of me." Chris shoved his plate away and leaned back. "I remember when we were in high school, all the guys wanted a date with *you*. There must be a special guy in your life, right?"

"Of course there is," I said, sounding defensive. What did he care? I didn't like the turn this conversation had taken, especially since I hadn't had a date in months, but no way would I admit that to *him*. "I'm just too busy to think about marriage."

I pushed back my chair and stood, anxious to get the kitchen cleaned up so I could retreat to Ellie's room and read a book or lurk on Facebook—anything to get away from his scrutiny. It made me nervous the way his brows furrowed, as though he found my single status perplexing.

His iPhone chirped again. Somebody really wanted him to answer his or her text message. I leaned over and tried to look at the screen, but he placed his hand over it. "Aren't you going to answer that?"

He rose from the table and picked up the iPhone. "No, it's not important," he said in a tense voice and turned it off. "I'm going to watch a movie."

Without another word, he left the room.

Chapter Three

After Chris went upstairs to the den, I scraped the dishes and scrubbed down the kitchen. Since he made lunch, I figured he shouldn't have to stick around to clean up, too. Besides, the way he stalked off indicated I'd touched on a sensitive subject. Whoever wanted his attention had ticked him off in a very personal way. I thought about it as I wiped off the table and decided it must be either the press or an event organizer who wouldn't stop hounding him.

I hauled all of my gear up to Ellie's room and dropped it on the bed. All, except for my kitten. I placed his tote on the floor and lifted him out, allowing him to run where he pleased. The kitten decided to follow me around, pouncing on my bare feet and sinking his needle-sharp claws into my toes. It hurt, but he had an enormous amount of bravado for such a little guy and he looked so cute that I couldn't bring myself to put him back in his bed. Instead, I shook him off gently with a laugh.

"Hey," I said and picked him up, tickling his round tummy. "You're a little toughie, aren't you? You sure like to play rough." I wondered what to name him. Toughie just didn't sound right, but my tired mind couldn't think of anything else. Lunch and a hot bath had really worn me out.

After organizing all of my things, I found a good romance novel and stretched out on the bed. I loved Ellie's room. She had a large bedroom on the upper level with her own private bath and a dorm-sized refrigerator. When we were teens, we used to get dolled up in her bathroom and sneak out of the house. We'd hoof it down to Sportsman's Bar by the lake and sit outside on the patio, listening to the band and drinking Cokes. And flirting, of course, with all of the cute boys staying at the resort next door. Through the years, Ellie had kept in touch with one of those boys, ended up eloping with him, and now had her first child on the way. As for me, well...

I have a business to run.

The thought surprised me. I'd never realized it before, but my attitude sounded bitter, maybe even a tad regretful. What had started as an exciting adventure, over the years had become a daily struggle and my enthusiasm had waned with my energy.

Burnout, that's what you have—exhaustion from going it alone. Now that you've established yourself in the business, you wonder if it was all worth it.

"That's nonsense," I argued aloud, "My business is doing better than ever. I did over thirty weddings last year." But the words sounded strange, as though I'd been talking about someone else.

I opened my book and started to read, brushing off my negative thoughts.

A couple of hours later, I heard the downstairs door slam as Chris left the house. He never bothered to tell me where he was going or what time he'd be back, but I guess he didn't need to explain anything to me. I just hoped he didn't stay out too late because I didn't like the idea of hearing someone coming into the house in the wee hours of the morning.

At ten o'clock, I went downstairs and threw a couple of oak logs on the hot coals to rejuvenate the fire. I opened a bottle of Cabernet and spread a thick blanket on the sofa to burrow under as I watched the news.

This is what I had planned on doing all along—curling up on the sofa in front of the fire with a good bottle of wine, but for some strange reason, it seemed like an empty exercise now.

"Here, Rex," I called, wanting company. "Come here, boy."

I never thought I'd turn to a dog for companionship, but then, I never thought I'd find myself drawn to my childhood nemesis, either. Oddly, my life had come full circle today.

****

Chris came home at midnight, his boots thundering as he crossed the screen porch and burst through the back door. He looked surprised to see me on the sofa watching a movie. Rex lay sleeping on the floor next to the sofa, his long legs, and body sprawled across the carpet.

"I thought you'd be in bed by now," Chris said as he pulled off his coat and shoved it into the closet.

Rex came to life and bolted toward his master, dancing around Chris to show his excitement.

I responded with a wry chuckle. "If I had, I'd be fully awake now. You made enough noise to wake the dead."

He toed off his snowy boots and walked toward the fireplace to warm his hands. "I went to Sportsman's Bar to have a few beers with some of my old friends." He gestured toward my wine bottle. "If I'd known you were going to sit here and drink by yourself, I'd have asked you to come with me."

"That would be a first." I laughed. "You and me, tying one on."

"The last time we saw each other we were too young to drink," he said, giving Rex a couple of pats on the back.

I sat up and swung my legs over the side of the sofa. "If I remember right, that never stopped you."

He grinned and gestured toward the ceiling, referring to the lounge directly above us. "Who could resist an entire kitchen stocked with booze? Of course, I never got caught helping myself, but I knew I had to eventually change my ways or I'd never make it into major league baseball."

"Don't we all?" I threw off the blanket and rose to my feet. "Realize the need to change our ways, I mean."

"You haven't." He walked toward me. "You're sweet and honest and genuine. You've always possessed all the right qualities. Why do you think all of the guys in school fought over you?"

My mouth gaped. I had no recollection of anyone fighting over me. What in the heck brought that on? I knew he'd been drinking, but I'd seen him under the influence before and he'd never talked to me like *that*.

His iPhone beeped in his pocket. I wanted to throw that annoying thing outside into a snowbank, but my irritation subsided when he looked deep into my eyes. His hand gently reached up and cradled the nape of my neck. "Don't ever change, Annabelle." His head bent forward and my heart jumped into my throat as I realized he meant to kiss me. To my surprise, I froze, unable to resist. Deep down, I wondered what it would be like to taste his lips upon mine. Would one kiss entice me to want more or would it simply annoy me, as he had always managed to do?

Suddenly, the oak logs in the fireplace shifted and one rolled against the screen. The noise distracted us, causing us both to look toward it. Smoke began pouring out one end of the log, flowing heavily into the air.

I bent over in a coughing fit and staggered toward the stairs while Chris grabbed the fireplace tools to shove the log deep into the brick-lined cavity so the smoke would go up the chimney. At the same time, the smoke detector went off with the intensity of a severe weather alarm. Chris opened a window to bring in some fresh air then pulled the cover off the alarm to disable it until the smoke cleared.

Using the incident as an excuse to escape, I covered my ears and climbed the stairs to Ellie's bedroom. Once inside the room, I closed the door and collapsed on the bed. I needed to catch my breath, but not from breathing in the strong odor of a burning oak log. The realization of what almost happened between Chris and I had shocked me. My heart fluttered at the thought; at the same time, the voice of my conscience spoke loud and clear.

You're a fool if you allow him to start something he doesn't intend to finish.

He had a girlfriend. Christopher Stone *always* had a girlfriend. I'd seen him on the cover of more than one gossip magazine with women whose beauty and charisma I could never duplicate. Allowing him to kiss me would be the ultimate joke—on me.

Armed with fresh determination, I locked my bedroom door and set my mind to get through the next four days without any more incidents. If he tried to kiss me again, he'd have to leave. I never took any guff from the boys in high school and I didn't intend to take any from him.

Chapter Four

The next morning, I took my time getting out of bed. The kitten woke me early, wanting to eat. I poured milk into his dish from a small glass I'd stored in Ellie's refrigerator and allowed him to roam freely about the room as I went back to sleep. He had a litter box to do his business and a blanket to keep him warm, but when I awoke, I found him sleeping next to my head on the pillow. I didn't want any piddle on the bedding so I put him in his litter box as soon as he stirred.

When I finally dressed and went downstairs, the stale odor of smoke still clung to everything in the living room. The fireplace, now cold and dark, needed cleaning to get rid of the burnt odor. Passing through, I scrunched my nose at the acrid stench and decided it would be a good job for Chris.

He sat at the kitchen table, drinking a large mug of coffee and surfing on his laptop. Next to his chair, Rex sprawled out on the floor, snoring. "Good morning, sunshine," Chris said without looking up. "There's a fresh pot of coffee on the counter."

The nickname "Sunshine" didn't sit well with me, but I let it go. The word conjured up past conversations with him, and not pleasant ones, either, but I'd decided it didn't matter anymore. As I'd indicated to him last night, people gradually changed their ways and I had changed mine. Privately, I had made up my mind not to let him get to me any longer, in any capacity, and planned to act as if our near-kiss had never happened.

I filled a large mug and took a sip. He made a mean cup of coffee; I had to admit. The brew was so hot it scalded my tongue and so strong it could strip paint.

Chris looked up from his laptop. "That's some pretty good French roast, isn't it?"

"Yeah," I said, barely able to mouth the word. "I need some flavored cream."

He drank his coffee black, so I knew I wouldn't find any liquid creamer in the refrigerator, but I looked anyway. Needing something to dilute the taste, I rummaged through the cabinets to see if I could find any of the powdered stuff. I found a can of cinnamon, sliced almonds, and instant pancake mix but no creamer. Then I saw a bag of Toll House chocolate chips and pulled it out, tossing it on the counter with the rest of the stuff.

Chris immediately zeroed in on the bag. "Are they still fresh? I mean, no mouse holes chewed in the plastic or any bugs, right?"

I picked it up and examined it. "No, it looks fine to me."

He sprung from his chair. "I'm in the mood for some homemade cookies—how about you?"

I shrugged, thinking I had already planned to spend the day putting up Christmas decorations. Flipping the bag over, I read the recipe. "We're short a few ingredients."

"Like what?"

I pulled open the refrigerator door again and looked inside. "Just to make sure we don't run out of groceries until Friday, it looks like we're going to need butter, eggs, and probably some fresh brown sugar.

We don't want any dark sugar lumps in the cookies." I checked the cabinet with baking supplies and found a can of baking soda that looked usable and a small bottle of vanilla. In a lower cabinet, I found large Tupperware containers of flour and white sugar.

Chris reached across the table for his keys and his wallet. His iPhone lay next to his laptop, hooked to the charger. He checked his messages but left it plugged in. "Is that it?"

I saw the searching look in his eyes and knew his question referred to more than the ingredients.

"*Yes.*" No way did I even want to discuss what happened last night much less try it again.

He shut down his computer. "I'm going to the store. Is there anything else you need?"

I shook my head, preferring to do my shopping on Thursday for the weekend.

After he left the house, I noticed his iPhone still lying on the table connected to the charger. It hadn't chirped once all morning and I wondered if his harasser had given up.

Common sense warned me to leave it alone, but I wanted to know who kept bugging him to the point of making him upset. I slid the iPhone toward me and gingerly picked it up. Even though Chris had already driven away, I glanced out the window, checking for fresh tire tracks in the snow to make sure he'd gone. Invading someone else's privacy went against my better judgment, but I couldn't stand not knowing.

Just this one time, I thought. *Then I'll mind my own business.*

I looked at the screen and located the green message button in the upper left-hand corner. My finger hovered over it for a moment as I gave myself a second chance to do the right thing and put the iPhone down. Unfortunately, curiosity got the better part of me. I touched the message button and the list instantly populated onto the screen. I scanned it with curiosity, amazed to see that every text message came from the same person, R.S. No one else had texted Chris in days.

I squinted at the picture on all of the texts and nearly swallowed my tongue. Chris had been receiving messages from Riley Sutton, the most fickle, most notoriously temperamental pop music diva *ever*. Her tantrums were legendary. She had a reputation for flipping out, often completely melting down over having to wait ten minutes for anything—luggage, food, a limo—you name it.

Riley lived on Twitter and posted selfies of doing everything except going to the bathroom. She always had at least one feud going with another female star and tended to write ugly songs about her breakup with nearly every guy she used—ahem, became estranged.

I'd been so busy lately catching up on paperwork for my tax man I hadn't looked at any of the gossip magazines online and I didn't know Chris and Riley were dating. If you could call it that. Riley tended to treat her boyfriends like glorified servants. Hail to the Drama Queen!

Most of the messages from the last several days remained unopened, but now I knew why. She and Chris were having issues. Well, *duh*. I noticed he'd opened the last message. He'd received it last night and I wanted to read it, but my conscience *really* bothered me now. Though I'd done my share of gossiping, I had never eavesdropped on someone else's private conversation like this before.

I had decided against reading it when my finger accidentally made contact with the iPhone and the message opened up.

Last chance. Call me. NOW.

On the surface, the message told me nothing, yet what it implied spoke volumes. Riley Sutton thought threatening Chris would force him to act, but she didn't know him very well. He possessed a stubborn streak that didn't bend unless he wanted it to. Something had obviously gone wrong between him and Riley, causing a rift, at least from his point of view. She wanted him to admit responsibility by calling her, but he refused to back down.

I smiled. The diva had met her match.

Placing the iPhone back on the table, I went about the business of dragging all of the Christmas decorations out of storage and stacking them in the family room upstairs. That room, situated next to the lounge, had a solid glass wall with a huge open fireplace. The girls would spend the entire weekend up there, sipping wine and enjoying the magnificent view.

Chris walked in an hour later with several bags of groceries.

"What's all this," I said, staring at the bags. "I sent you to the store for three things and you come back with half their inventory."

He pulled two frozen pizzas and a tray of frosted sweet rolls out of the first bag. "I guess I got a little carried away, but these look really good, don't they?"

I burst out laughing. I couldn't help it. "Did you remember to get the stuff to make the cookies?"

"Sure," he said, ripping open the package of rolls and pulling one out. "I also got you some of that fancy creamer you were looking for in the refrigerator."

How sweet, I thought, but I didn't say so. Instead, I emptied all of the bags and put the food away except for the ingredients I sent him for in the first place. Once I finished, I set the temperature in the oven and started reading the recipe on the back of the Toll House Morsels package.

"Here." I handed Chris a huge green Tupperware mixing bowl and a wooden spoon. The bowl contained two sticks of cold butter, sugar, and vanilla. "I'm the ingredients coordinator and you've got the muscles so you're the ingredients mixer."

"But I don't know how to bake—"

"You can do it." I pointed a finger at him. "Just stir it until it's nice and creamy."

It took him a few minutes to cream the butter, but when he'd finished, I dropped in two eggs and had him stir some more. Then I had him fold in the dry ingredients—slowly—and finally the chocolate chips.

I set a cookie sheet on the table and handed him two spoons. "Scoop out a walnut-sized ball of dough with one spoon and use the other to scrape it off and drop it onto the pan."

He set down the spoons and looked at me as though I'd lost my mind. "No. You're the cookie dropper. I'm the cookie *taster*."

"All right." I let out a dramatic sigh and started dropping small balls of dough onto the sheet.

All of a sudden, something hit me in the center of my forehead. "What the—" Rubbing it off with the back of my hand, I looked up and saw Chris staring at me with a twinkle in his eye and a dough-filled spoon aimed right at my chest. At first, I reacted in my usual way, by getting mad, but then I decided what the heck, two could play at this game. "Up to your old tricks are you, Stone?" I grabbed a ball of dough off the cookie sheet and lobbed it at him. He ducked, laughing, and the ball hit the window. Then he shot one at me. The next thing I knew, we were catapulting dough at each other like a couple of teenagers.

Rex watched the chunks fly through the air and gobbled them up as soon as they hit the floor.

"Wait!" I snatched the bowl away and covered it protectively with my arms. "Rex is not supposed to have chocolate." I looked at the dog, sitting at Chris' feet, his tail thumping wildly. "I hope he doesn't get the poops from raw cookie dough." I gave Chris a sly smile, garnering satisfaction at seeing him wince. "I'm not the one who's going to be cleaning *that* out of the carpet."

We called a truce and I resumed spooning out the dough.

Out of the blue, Chris said, "I'm surprised you're still speaking to me."

I shoved the pan into the oven and set the timer. "Why?"

He leaned his elbows on the table. "When we were kids, you would have been spitting mad over this."

I grabbed the wooden spoon and shook it in his face. "What makes you think I'm not mad now? You hit me with cookie dough."

"You can't laugh and be mad at the same time." He grinned. "And by the way, you're a lousy shot. You'd make a terrible ballplayer."

"Oh, yeah? Well, you make a lousy baking partner." I grabbed a roll of paper towels and a bottle of cleaning spray. "But you can make it up to me by wiping dough off the walls."

Chris attempted to clean the walls while I baked the cookies. When the first batch came out, I had to practically arm-wrestle him to keep his fingers out of the pan to let them cool long enough to handle. After I baked all the cookies and cleaned up the kitchen, I carried a plate upstairs for Chris and me to munch on while we put together the Christmas tree.

I tried to concentrate on what we were doing, but I couldn't get that text message from Riley Sutton out of my mind.

"So, what's it like dating a pop star," I asked as I started to string lights on the seven-foot artificial tree.

"That depends on what you want to know." Chris casually took the lights from me and reached up, starting the string at the very top. He kept his voice even, but I sensed his manner tensing.

"Is it exciting?" I opened a box of glass ornaments and began hanging them on the branches.

"It's an unreal world."

Taken aback by the sharpness in his reply, I paused. "What do you mean?"

He answered with a cynical laugh. "The last girl I dated partied every night," he said as he began winding the lights around the tree. "She slept until noon then spent the afternoon getting her hair and makeup done to go out again. She had the entire top floor of her mansion converted into a salon and a walk-in closet the size of a department store so she didn't have to leave the house to get ready."

"Sounds like a dream."

He snorted. "Sounds pointless to me."

"I thought you liked that kind of life."

"Yeah, it was fun for a while, but I can't see myself living like that permanently. Someday my career in baseball is going to end and I'll be just a regular guy again, looking to get married and have kids. That lifestyle of constant partying doesn't leave room for anything resembling normal." We stood facing each other. The top of my head reached his chin. "Wouldn't you like to settle down one of these days? Don't you get tired of being single?"

Wow. I never thought I'd hear talk like that coming out of *his* mouth.

"Of course," I said, "but finding the person who's right for you isn't easy."

He sighed. "I agree."

We finished decorating the tree and putting up all of the decorations by late afternoon. Too tired to cook, I heated the oven again and put in one of the pizzas Chris had brought home from the store. While the pizza baked, I went upstairs to my room to feed my kitten but when I arrived, I found the door ajar and my kitten missing.

I searched the entire house, looking under beds and dressers, behind the sofas, and around the Christmas tree. The little guy had literally vanished. My nerves were on edge with worry.

I ran back upstairs where Chris sat watching television in the den. "Have you seen my kitten? He must have gotten out of my room."

He shook his head. "Don't worry. He's probably sleeping somewhere. He'll turn up."

But I did worry. I should have heard him mewing with hunger. I began to tear the house apart again, looking under cushions, inside the closets, and searched my bedroom once more, but he didn't turn up. I had one more place to check—Chris' room. I didn't like the idea of snooping around his private domain, but I needed to make sure the kitten hadn't gone in there.

His bedroom door stood ajar so I pushed it open. I flipped on the light and looked around. Pictures of his fishing and hunting trips covered the walls including a couple of stuffed walleye and a deer trophy centered above the headboard of his bed. Rex sat on his fuzzy plaid bed in the corner with his front legs extended and his nose touching his paws. His gaze followed me as I turned over the blankets and pillows on Chris' bed, picked up the clothes on the floor, and peeked inside the closet. Rex's reticence struck me as odd. That dog never settled down.

"What's the matter, boy?" I walked over to him and reached down to scratch his ears. "Got a tummy ache from eating raw cookie dough?" He shrunk away from my hand and as his head moved, I saw a small mound of gray and black striped fur curled up under his chin.

"Chris! Chris!"

My voice must have bordered on hysteria because I heard Chris' feet thundering down the hallway and taking the stairs two at a time to reach the lower level. He burst into his bedroom and looked around, his face stricken, as though he feared the worst. "What's wrong? Did you find the kitten?"

Panicking, I pointed to Rex. *"He* has my kitten!"

Chris stared at me, disbelieving. "What?"

"Rex has my kitten!" I dropped to my knees and pointed to the dark spot under the dog's chin. "He's right there, but I don't know if Rex will allow me to take him. Hurry, pull him out, and see if he's still alive!"

Chris slipped his hand under Rex's jaw and lifted the dog's head. The kitten lay sleeping peacefully in between the dog's legs. Rex whined and pulled away then began licking the kitten's face with his long, pink tongue.

"He's not hurting it." Chris nudged the tiny body with his knuckle and the kitten mewed. "I think he's protecting it."

I stared at the odd pair and realized I no longer owned a pet. My tiny kitten had been adopted by a huge but lovable, German shepherd.

Chapter Five

Wednesday, December 12th

"Hold it, right there. Say *cheese*."

I stood behind my camera on the tripod and peered through the lens. We were upstairs in the living room shooting photos where we had the best light. I had talked Chris into allowing me to take a couple of practice shots of him before we tackled Rex, but he wouldn't agree until I promised to frame the best one and wrap it so he could give it to his mother for Christmas. I took a dozen shots of him in front of the Christmas tree and in front of the crackling fire in the open fireplace.

My motive for getting a good shot of him wasn't entirely unselfish. I wanted to give one to Ellie for Christmas, too. She and I always competed to see who could give each other the most unusual gift. I figured a framed image of her twin brother with his beautiful dog at their cabin would be a huge surprise, but one that she would love.

Rex lay by the Christmas tree, patiently watching over the kitten. Once Chris accepted the fact that he now owned a dog *and* a cat, he named the little guy Turbo. And boy, did Turbo live up to his name. Turbo had no fear of Rex whatsoever. He skittered around the dog, arching his back and making swipes with his paw, coaxing Rex to play. Whenever Rex would get his nose close enough, Turbo would pounce on his face, biting and scratching him. With amazing patience, Rex would gently brush him off.

"Chris, let's get a few shots of you kneeling next to Rex in front of the tree," I said and pointed to the spot where I wanted them to pose.

"Come here, Rex." Chris patted his thigh. "Come on, boy."

But Rex wouldn't move. He had no interest in posing. He wanted to be with the cat.

Chris walked over to the dog and picked up Turbo then took his place in front of the tree. Rex followed and sat next to him, but wouldn't look at the camera. His gaze focused solely on Turbo.

"Give Turbo to me." I took the cat and walked behind the camera again. I held Turbo above the camera and made a kissing sound to get Rex to perk up his ears. Instead, he ran toward me and jumped on me, thinking I wanted to play using the cat as bait.

Chris shook his head. "This isn't going to work. Rex is too distracted."

I thought for a moment, strategizing on how I could get the dog to sit still. "I have an idea. I'll put the cat on the sofa with a saucer of milk so he's out of the way. Then I'll set the timer on the camera and lay on the floor, holding Rex from the other side so he can't move. I'll try to stay low enough so I'm not seen, but if my arms or hands show up in the picture, I'll just crop them out."

I ran downstairs and filled a saucer with milk. When I got back upstairs, Rex detected the milk and followed me to the sofa. "Get the dog," I said to Chris and scooped up the cat. I set Turbo on the sofa with his mid-morning snack and went back to my camera to set the auto-timer while Chris and Rex took their places.

"Ready? Once I press the shutter, we have ten seconds to get this right." At Chris' nod, I set the camera and hurried over to Rex. I dropped to the floor and gripped my hands around his front legs, but he wanted no part of this picture. He slipped out of my hands, jumped over me, and bounded toward the sofa.

Out of ideas, I groaned in frustration.

Suddenly, Chris' hands spanned my midriff and hauled me to a sitting position. He pulled me to his side and circled both arms around me, drawing me close as he pressed his cheek to mine. "Say cheese."

The strong, yet gentle pressure of his arms surrounding me caught me by surprise. My pulse raced. I couldn't breathe. My thoughts jumbled into an incoherent blur and I stared numbly into the camera as his hard, muscular body leaned into mine, the rough texture of his jaw grazing my soft skin.

I barely had time to look into the camera before the flash went off.

"Couldn't see wasting a perfectly good picture," he murmured in my ear. I didn't know for sure, but that low purr in his voice told me what he was thinking and it wasn't about the photo. Panicking, I turned away, not giving him a chance to kiss me.

Without a word, he released me and rose to his feet then reached down and offered his hand. I slipped my palm into his and stood up.

I sensed he wanted to say something, but his closeness unsettled me. I turned my back to him and walked over to the camera, putting all my effort into checking the finished picture. It stunned me even more to see us together as a couple, but I pretended not to notice anything unusual. Instead, I busied myself adjusting the tripod even though it didn't require attention. I needed something to do to keep my shaking hands busy until I calmed down.

After several tries, we managed to get Rex to settle down long enough to get a decent shot of him and Chris—but only one. Chris had to sit with Turbo on his knee, needle-sharp claws and all, to get Rex to behave.

Later, I downloaded the images to my laptop and went through them to select the best ones for Chris. When I came upon the photo of him and me together sitting cheek to cheek, I stared, stunned. Photos didn't lie and this one conveyed more about me than I cared to admit.

My eyes shone and my effortless smile was radiant, expressing a level of joy I hadn't seen in myself in a long time. How could that be when I was experiencing such inner turmoil? I stared at the image some more, trying to understand the sudden change in me. I looked so natural in Chris' arms, as though I belonged there.

The thought alarmed me.

Get a grip, girl. Don't make this into something it isn't. You've called a truce with an old nemesis and you're enjoying each other's company for a couple of days, but he's leaving on Friday and you probably won't see him again for a long, long time. He'll go back to his life and you'll go back to yours. Let it go...

Reality had set in and I realized I needed to stop entertaining such impractical thoughts. I selected the best shots, emailed them to Chris then closed the laptop and went to my room. I stayed there most of the day, reading, resting, and thinking about my future—the reason I'd arrived a couple of days early in the first place. There was one thing this time of reflection had taught me for sure. I had become so singularly focused on building my business by working myself ragged that I'd gradually lost sight of how out of touch I was with my feelings—until a simple near-kiss had me running for the exit. Christopher Stone had no clue what he'd done, but by dangling the temptation in front of me, he'd opened my eyes. And what I saw filled my heart with despair.

I was tired, lonely, and totally unsure of my future.

Chapter Six

Thursday, December 13th

On Thursday, I arose early and spent the better part of the day cleaning the house. I had bedding to wash, vacuuming to do, both the kitchen and the lounge floors needed mopping and I had four bathrooms to scrub. Later that afternoon, I went into town to buy my share of the groceries for the weekend and a bottle of my favorite wine.

It had snowed during the night. Chris shoveled the sidewalks and used the snowblower to clean out the driveway then spent the rest of the day in the den, handling personal business over the phone and on the Internet. As I finished putting away the groceries, he appeared in the kitchen with his duffel bag, wearing jeans and a maroon sweater.

"I'm leaving in a couple of minutes," he said quietly. "I have to meet with my agent tomorrow before I join my buddies at the hospital so I'm staying at my folk's place tonight."

Though I tried not to let the news affect me, I experienced a profound sadness at the thought of him leaving.

"Thanks for hanging out with me. I've really enjoyed the last few days," I said, forcing myself to sound cheerful. I didn't want to admit it, but the thought of being all alone in this big house tonight—without him—filled my heart with loneliness.

"Thank *you*," he said, "for the cookies and the photos." He flashed a handsome grin. "And for Turbo. Rex thanks you most of all."

I knew Turbo would be happier with Chris and Rex, but I'd developed a special bond with him and now I regretted letting him go. I blinked hard, not wanting Chris to see my silly sentimentality.

He hesitated for a moment, a questioning look in his eyes as if waiting for me to respond.

I didn't move. I didn't know what else to say.

"Goodbye, Annabelle."

"Goodbye, Chris."

A few minutes later, I stood at the window watching the lights of his car cut a blue-white swath through the night as he drove away.

I wandered through the house, listless and depressed. I'd had issues with my life when I arrived here, but they were ten times worse now. Not only did I wish I could skip the weekend with my girlfriends, but I also dreaded going back to work next week, too. The sad truth haunted me and I couldn't ignore it any longer. I'd used my profession to fulfill my life's desire and it had failed me miserably. I loved photography but deep in my heart, I'd known for a long time it was a poor substitute for what I really needed—to love a man and to be loved in return.

That desire had lain dormant for years, buried under layers of appointments, bridal fairs, and extensive "To Do" lists. Knowing what I knew now, I'd give it all up in a moment if presented with the chance.

I walked into the den and immediately sensed Chris' presence. The local newspaper he'd been reading lay on the oak coffee table next to his empty Coke bottle and an open bag of chips.

I curled up on the beige sofa with a thick blanket. Faint traces of his cologne clung to the soft-textured upholstery. My eyes filled with mist. I missed him already.

Chapter Seven

Friday, December 14th

The next morning, I awoke stiff and sore with the rising sun glaring in my eyes. Something sharp poked me in the hip. I sat up, rubbed the tender spot in my skin, and bumped the object with my hand. It had slipped down inside the sofa, wedged between the pillow-style backrest and the thick cushions. I reached in between the cushions and pulled out a long, thin photo album that belonged to Ellie. I'd seen this blue book, faded and worn, in the den on the bookcase when I searched around for Turbo. One corner of the book had aligned with the center edge of the cushions and my hip must have pushed against it all night, causing my discomfort. A couple of yellowed pages fell out and my gaze fell on old pictures of Chris, Ellie, and me as teens.

I opened the book and reinserted the pages, but continued to leaf through it. Ellie had collected pictures of the three of us fishing, swimming, squirting each other with a garden hose, and eating picnic fare, but mostly they were a year-to-year chronicle of our summers hanging out at the cabin. Turning the page, I froze. Someone had taken a close-up shot of me at seventeen, sitting at a wooden picnic table in a pink bathing suit with my chin resting on my hands, and my long blonde hair draped about my shoulders. I didn't have a stitch of makeup on, but my face glowed. My youthful smile radiated, displaying a bit of mischief and pure happiness. The picture itself didn't shock me. It was the youthful scrawl below it that caused my heart to skip a beat. Underneath the photo, Chris had penned, "Princess Anna-belle. She's FROZEN." Ellie had scribbled it out, but I could still read it.

I sighed and slammed the book shut. "Why should this come as a surprise?" I asked myself aloud. "He wrote it to goad his sister about her best friend because he has always had a problem with me."

I lay back down and closed my eyes, too tired and disillusioned to get up. Sometime later, the house phone woke me up, but I didn't feel like talking to anyone so I let it go to the message machine. If it was for me, I'd call them back later. If not…

"Hey, Chris," a deep, masculine voice said. "It's Marty. I thought I'd catch you at home if I called this early. I just wanted to say I'm sorry about this girl who keeps breakin' your heart. I hear ya, buddy. Like I told you the other night, there was a girl *back in the day* who did the same thing to me so I know where you're coming from. Give me a call back if you want to talk about it over a beer. Catch ya…"

My brain went into a tailspin. It didn't take a genius to discern that Marty was referring to me. If Chris had liked me *back in the day*, why had he picked on me so much? More importantly, why hadn't he told *me* how he felt instead of one of his close friends? I sat back and stared up at the knotty pine ceiling, trying to make sense of it all. Then I remembered his words last Monday night.

"You're sweet and honest and genuine. You've always possessed all the right qualities. Why do you think all of the guys in school fought over you?"

I couldn't fathom why he'd made that remark about all of the boys in school, but now I understood. He'd watched other boys compete for my attention, knowing I wouldn't have anything romantic to do with him.

I recalled how he'd placed his hand on the curve of my neck, looked deep into my eyes, and said, *"Don't ever change, Annabelle."*

He still thought of me as that sweet, innocent girl he knew back in high school.

Rising from the sofa, I stumbled down the hallway to Ellie's room to locate my phone. I found it at the bottom of my purse, but it wouldn't turn on. I hadn't thought about using it in days so I'd forgotten to charge it.

I made a pot of coffee, took a shower, and fixed my makeup while I waited for my phone to build up enough of a charge to make a call. At nine o'clock, I turned it on and dialed his number. I'd written it on a pad in the kitchen that day he'd gone to the store to get groceries.

He answered it on the second ring.

"Annabelle, what's wrong?"

The sound of his deep voice rumbling in my ear made my hands shake and I almost dropped my phone.

"I need to ask you something." My voice quaked so much I could hardly speak.

After a long, awkward pause, he responded warily, "Okay..."

Might as well just say it and get it over with.

So, I blurted it out. "Why did you put a live snake down my shirt?"

"What?"

"Tell me. I want to know."

He didn't answer right away. Then he sighed and said, "I wanted you to notice me."

The signs of attraction through his desperate attempts to get my attention had been there all along. Growing up, I had been just too immature, too blind to see it.

My head began to spin. I collapsed on Ellie's bed, hoping to make it stop. "Why didn't you just tell me you liked me? What made you think harassing me would work instead?"

He must have been in his car because I heard Christmas music in the background. "I tried to talk to you," he said gently, "but you kept ignoring me so I gave up. Eventually, it seemed easier to get your attention by making you mad."

I couldn't believe this. He'd pulled tricks on me simply to get my attention? "*Why*?"

"You really don't know, do you? I had a crush on you, Annabelle, all through high school. Now, are you satisfied? We're playing the same old game—You're stomping on my heart while I'm groveling at your feet."

In my mind, none of this made sense. He'd just confessed he'd had a crush on me for years, but he couldn't tell me about it even though he saw me nearly every day at school. Then we graduated and I never saw him again until three days ago. "If you had it so bad for me, why did you just let me go? Why didn't you find some other way to communicate your feelings to me?"

"What was the point? You made it plain you didn't like me. I finally got it through my thick head and left you alone."

I stared at the ceiling, completely baffled. "You never asked me if I liked you."

He uttered a wry chuckle. "We're going in circles, Annabelle. Nothing will ever change between you and me, will it?"

"Yes, it will!" I practically shouted into the phone. "Do you like me, *Christopher Stone*?

The only word that came to mind in the wake of his obvious pause was "pregnant" because his answer held the power to birth an entirely new beginning in my life.

"I love you, Annabelle," he said gently. "I always have."

My eyes rushed with tears and I knew at that moment that I loved him, too. I loved everything about him, from his wacky sense of humor to his heart for kids. I wanted to reply to that properly, but definitely *not* over the phone. "I wish you were here, telling me this in person."

"I tried several times." His voice sounded tired and sad. "You rejected me outright so I backed off. I couldn't handle being pushed away again."

What a mess. He had a charity function after lunch. I had a girls' weekend starting at five o'clock. About a hundred and fifty miles lay between us. Why did my life always go this way?

"Come to Minneapolis and I *will* tell you in person," he said. "I'll tell you so many times you'll never forget it."

My heart wrenched. I wanted to tell him, yes, but the only reply I could manage amounted to a strangled sob.

"Look, if you leave now and the traffic is decent, you'll get here just about on time. Please, Annabelle, I want you here with me at the hospital. I need you here by my side. You and me, we'll be a dynamic team. I'll hand out the gifts and you'll take shots of the kids."

I heard the desperation in his voice and squeezed my eyes shut. Mascara-laden tears ran down my cheeks.

"This is what you were made for and *you know it*."

The thought of working with children in need with Chris sounded like a dream come true. Suddenly, I never wanted to deal with fussy, demanding brides ever again. I pulled the phone charging cord out of the wall, slid off the bed, and walked into the bathroom. "I have to wash my face and then I'll leave." I grabbed a tissue to wipe my nose. "Where do I park?"

"I'll meet you at the west ramp. I'll find two spaces and park over the line so no one else can park there until you come. I'm on the way to meet with my agent now, but as soon as I get to the hospital, I'll text you which level I'm on."

I had the water running, the phone on speaker mode, and creamy cleanser covering my face. "I'm out of here in less than five minutes."

"I'll be waiting," he said eagerly. "I lo—"

"Hold that thought!" I wrung out the washcloth and vigorously scrubbed my face. "I want the next time to be in person."

I hung up and finished washing my face then added a little mascara to my red, swollen eyes. Grabbing my keys and my camera case, I headed for the closet to get my coat. Hopefully, my face would be back to normal by the time I reached Minneapolis because if I didn't stop crying, I would be scaring a lot of sick kids.

My car reached the south ramp in two hours and five minutes. I didn't speed...well, not enough to get pulled over by the highway patrol. Chris had found two spots together in the ramp and it didn't long to locate his dark blue BMW. He moved his car over and I parked mine.

I'd barely pulled out the keys and disconnected my seatbelt before my door flew open and Chris' strong arms reached in and pulled me out. He circled his arms around me and held me tight, kissing me with so much force he pushed me back against the car. I slid my arms around his neck and joined my mouth to his, giving myself completely to him. The heat of his strong, lean body melded with mine, causing my heart to pound so hard in my chest I could barely breathe. My stomach quivered, causing a giddiness I hadn't experienced since my first kiss. In a way, this was my first kiss—my first *real* kiss of true love. And to think, I could have experienced this years ago...

"I should have kissed you a long time ago," I whispered, "but I never thought it could feel like *this*."

"I've wanted to do this to you my entire adult life," he murmured in my ear and kissed me again. "Just so you know, I plan on doing it for the *rest* of my life."

Making out in a hospital parking ramp didn't exactly meet the description of a glamorous or romantic location, but I didn't care if we were in the middle of the freeway at rush hour. My heart had never been this close to bursting with joy.

He pulled back, just enough to look deeply into my eyes. "I love you, Annabelle. I love you, Annabelle. I love you—"

"I love you, Chris." Then I silenced him with another kiss. I loved hearing it, but showing me worked far better.

He slid one hand around the base of my neck and the other hand under my chin, lifting my face to look into my eyes again. "I've loved you all my life. Ever since we were kids, you've always been in the back of my mind. I'm sorry I've failed you. I just didn't know how to communicate with girls back then."

My eyes stung with tears, but I willed them to stop. "It doesn't matter. We're here, now, and we're mature enough to know what it takes to make a good relationship into a great one."

He kissed the tip of my nose, resting his forehead against mine. "When you arrived at the house on Monday, being near you scared me so much that I nearly packed up and left. But deep in my heart, I knew I had to stick it out because I might never get another shot to be with you. I wanted so badly to make you want me. I even left my phone on the table on purpose when I went to the store, hoping you'd see the text messages from Riley Sutton and get jealous. Yesterday, I couldn't take it anymore and I had to leave. If I'd known years ago what I know now, we'd be married and living happily ever after."

The Riley Sutton comment made me smile, but I took the rest of it to heart. "We *are* living happily ever after from this moment on. It's never too late to start over."

Chris' iPhone chirped in his coat pocket.

I sighed. "Please, throw that thing away."

He began to laugh. "How about I just change my phone number and delete my Twitter account?" His face quickly sobered. "I called Riley right after I talked to you and told her to forget she ever knew me. Then I uploaded the picture of you and me to Twitter. She's tweeting stuff about us like mad, looking for public revenge."

I shrugged. "Who cares what she says about us? She may be rich and famous, but in reality, she's nothing but a self-centered twit. All I'm concerned with is getting back to Breezy Point by five o'clock tonight."

"Don't worry." He opened the car door for me to retrieve my purse and equipment. "I'll make sure you get back in time. I'll drive you myself."

I slung the bags over my shoulder and shut the car door. "How are you going to get back to the cities without your car?"

"I'm not," he said with a sexy grin as he slid his arm around me and we began to walk toward the elevators. "I'll get a room at the resort for the weekend. On Sunday night, when the girls are gone, I'll come back to the house and we'll have the place *all to ourselves...*"

I couldn't wait.

The End

A note from Denise…

Thank you for reading my sweet novella of true love. I love writing Christmas stories!

Rex is a fictional character, but the incident with him in Chapter Two is actually based on a true story. Many years ago, I had a dog named Chopper, half-shepherd, and half-something (Malamute, perhaps). He was huge and lovable, very strong, but he didn't know his own strength. There was an incident where he ran into the street, knocked down the neighbor lady, wolfed down her plate of spaghetti then licked her face. I can laugh about it now, but it wasn't so funny back then when the police got involved!

The part about Rex adopting Annabelle's kitten is also based on a true story. That one, however, came from a feature I read on the Internet. I always have at least one pet in every story because I love animals and I want my characters to love them, too. I believe every animal has its own unique personality.

If you enjoyed this story, please feel free to leave a review at the retailer where you purchased it. Reviews are how other readers find good books. If you'd like to know more about me or my other books, you can visit my website at **www.deniseannettedevine.com**

A Very Merry Christmas is also available on audiobook, too!

Check my website for more information and sales.

More Books by Denise Devine

Christmas Stories

Merry Christmas, Darling

A Christmas to Remember

A Merry Little Christmas

Once Upon a Christmas

Mistletoe and Wine – *Coming Soon!*

A Very Merry Christmas - Hawaiian Holiday Series

Bride Books

The Encore Bride

Lisa – Beach Brides Series

Ava – Perfect Match Series

Della – *Coming Soon!*

Moonshine Madness Series

Historical Suspense/Romance

The Bootlegger's Wife – Book 1

Guarding the Bootlegger's Widow – Book 2

The Bootlegger's Legacy – Book 3

The Nightingale Detective Agency – Book 4 – *Coming Soon!*

West Loon Bay Series – Small Town Romance

Small Town Girl – Book 1

Brown-Eyed Girl – Book 2

Country Girl – Book 3 - *Coming Soon!*

Cozy Mystery

Unfinished Business

Dark Fortune

~ Girl Friday Cozy Series ~

Shot in the Dark – Book 1

The Accidental Detective – *Coming Soon!*

Made in the USA
Monee, IL
11 January 2024

51617847R00085